Henry Astbury Leveson

The Camp Fire

Henry Astbury Leveson

The Camp Fire

ISBN/EAN: 9783337252090

Printed in Europe, USA, Canada, Australia, Japan

Cover: Foto ©Andreas Hilbeck / pixelio.de

More available books at **www.hansebooks.com**

THE CAMP-FIRE.

By H. A. L.,

("THE OLD SHEKARRY,")

AUTHOR OF "THE HUNTING GROUNDS OF THE OLD WORLD," ETC.

> While many a merry lay and many a song
> Cheer'd the rough road, we wish'd the rough road long.
> *Dr. Johnson.*

LONDON

A. E. BAILY AND CO., CORNHILL.

1866.

TO

LADY STRATFORD DE REDCLIFFE,

This Volume is Inscribed,

AS A TOKEN OF ESTEEM AND GRATITUDE

FROM

ONE OF THE MANY WOUNDED SOLDIERS

WHO EXPERIENCED

KINDNESS AND ATTENTION AT HER HANDS

WHEN LAID UP

IN THE MILITARY HOSPITAL AT SCUTARI.

INTRODUCTION.

THE following songs were written at different periods during the Russian War, when old friends and comrades used to meet nightly in each other's tents, or round the camp-fire, and every one was expected to sing when his turn came round. The poem of Inkermann was written whilst the Author was confined to his couch from severe wounds received at that battle, when, having but few books and no other means of amusement, time hung heavily on his hands. The task served to pass away many dull and weary hours; and besides proving a solace and recreation during a long and irksome confinement, it seemed to act as a sedative against continual pain, and prevented the mind from dwelling upon those series of heart-rending death-scenes, that of necessity were continually taking place in a crowded military hospital.

This poem having been commenced in a lady's album was not intended for the public eye, but simply to give personal friends some idea of a battle, and to show the incomparable conduct of the British soldier in one of the most sanguinary hand-to-hand fights in which our arms were ever engaged; but as many old companions in arms (whose better judgment has perhaps been biassed by their kindly feelings) have desired to have a copy of the work as a memento of those spirit-stirring days, the Author has laid it before the public, feeling convinced that the subject in itself possesses a certain interest which even the most unskilful hands cannot entirely extinguish.

After a lapse of nearly ten years these *waifs of the hour* have served a second time to divert the dull moments of indisposition; for the Author, (against whom Fortune appears to bear a grudge), having lately been again severely wounded whilst on duty upon the West Coast of Africa, has availed himself of his vacant hours to prepare the following pieces for the press.

> "Consider this: He hath been bred i' the wars
> Since he could draw a sword, and is ill-school'd
> In boulted language."

> "Do not take
> His rougher accents for malicious sounds,
> But, as I say, such as becomes a soldier."
>
> CORIOLANUS.

CONTENTS.

—◆—

INKERMANN.

MISCELLANEOUS POEMS AND SONGS.

INKERMANN.

CANTO THE FIRST.

———◦◦◦———

THE EVE OF THE BATTLE.

INKERMANN.

CANTO THE FIRST.

———◦◦———

THE EVE OF THE BATTLE.

"Coming events cast their shadows before."

———◦◦———

A WINT'RY sun had sunk to rest
Amid the vapours of the west;
And murky clouds of sombre grey
Seem'd to foretell a stormy day.
No gentle moon, or straggling star,
Shed light upon that field of war;
But dense mists roll'd upon the ground
And dreary darkness gather'd round.
Before me lay the leaguer'd town;
I mark'd its dusky bastions' frown,

E'en heard at times the vesper bells,

And shrill cries from the sentinels.[1]   ·

Malakoff's tower loom'd on high,

In dark relief against the sky ;

Whilst the Redan amidst the gloom

Lay grim and threatening as the tomb.

Our lines were hush'd in calm repose,

And all seem'd still amid our foes' ;

No voice, no sound, the silence broke,

Save when the guard a patrol spoke,

But the wind, whistling o'er the plain,   ‘

Assumed methought a wizard strain,[2]

As 'midst Tchernaya's hills it moan'd,

And like a dying mortal groan'd :

Now sweeping by, it struck the ear

Like something ominous and drear;

And, howling o'er dark Euxine's surge,

Murmur'd a low prophetic dirge.

What great events are on the gale ?[3]

Why does the wind thus sigh and wail?

Can it tell of coming sorrow ?

Does it warn us 'gainst the morrow ?

Is it that, with prophetic tone,

Departed loved ones who are gone

Still hover round, though out of sight,

Like guardian angels of the night ?

Have spirits of the dead the power

To warn us, ere our parting hour ;

Can friends we ne'er may see again

Shield us from danger or from pain?

Wild wind ! thy spell awoke a chord

Which for long years had slept unheard ;

For time had thrown a mist upon

The faded hopes of days bygone.

Yet in thy voice I heard a tone
That once was music all my own,
And o'er my burdened heart once more
Memory brought back days of yore;
Thy voice recalled the happy past,
A joyous time too bright to last,
And things which had been seem'd to rise
And flit before my spell-bound eyes;
Methought that one I loved was nigh,
For whispers soft as zephyr's sigh,
Oft seem'd to say, " We'll meet again
Where tears are not, nor grief, nor pain."
But she is gone whose voice to me
Was ever pleasing melody,
That made the wingèd moments seem
But as a bright and happy dream.
Time has not weakened memory's power;
My soul is weary since that hour;

Borne down by fate's relentless blow

There's nothing left to live for now.

Then, gentle wind, recall no more

The dream thou canst not now restore,

But let thy music seem to me

A requiem to her memory.

At last the gale which long had raged

Was for an interval assuaged;

But still a strange unearthly sound,

A low sad music, hovered round,

And on the night air seem'd to float

Like an Æolian harp's sweet note,

Whilst the ever murmuring sea

Accompanied the melody:

Receding now, it seem'd to glide

Far o'er the dark-blue heaving tide;

Again it rose, again it fell,

As if it breathed a last farewell.

Then lingering slowly o'er the bay,

Like an echo, it died away,

And the doom'd city seem'd to sleep

In death-like silence calm and deep.

Again was heard the convent's chime

Slowly pealing the hour of time,

Warning all " that a day had past,

That life will not for ever last."

It struck the ear of those who kept

The weary watch whilst comrades slept,

Like a solemn and well-known tone

They used to hear in years bygone,

When to the church they took their way,

With their friends on the Sabbath day,

To offer up an humble prayer
Ere stormy days of war and care.
As it rang at decline of day,
Who then dreamt of the coming fray?
Did those who on the morrow fell
Think it then sounded like a knell?

Though of a strange and wayward mood,
Inur'd to many a scene of blood,
I know not what came o'er my breast,
Or strange presentiment depressed;
Methought some peril seem'd to lour
Over my soul in that dark hour,
Though of a shape so undefined,
I scarce can call it back to mind;
Yet why dread evils that await,
Or heed foreshadowings of Fate?

For future hopes, that seem most fair,
Oft prove but castles in the air;
And if when brightest they deceive,
When they threaten shall we believe?
And shall a soldier reck or pine
Because life is not all sunshine?
Let him content him with the hour,
He must not heed though tempests lour.

Feeling alone and desolate,
Long thus I mused upon my fate.
In other lands my thoughts were fixed,
On bygone times, ere sorrow mixed
Within my cup the bitter draught,
Which to the very dregs I've quaffed.
Such were my thoughts as I strolled round
The height now Cathcart's burial-ground.

'Tis still midnight, and the moon is shrouded,

Dense mists are gathering, and stars are clouded;

Strange murmurs are heard on the freshening breeze —

Hark! Is it the wind that sighs through the trees?

Or is it the roll of the waves of ocean,

Lash'd by the storm-fiend in wild commotion?

Or is it the sound of the billows' roar

As they break in foam 'gainst the iron shore?

No! 'tis not the wind, nor waves 'gainst the coast;

'Tis the heavy tramp of a mighty host;

For the Muscovite hordes are pouring down

From the northern forts and the leaguer'd town,[4]

And a rushing sound is heard in the night

As bands of fierce horsemen, array'd for fight,

Gather in haste in the camp of the Czar,

Squadron on squadron, prepared for war.

No signal-trumpet blows, no clarion sings,

No sounding bugle through the night-air rings ;

Stilled and unbeaten is the martial drum,

A death-like silence reigns as on they come.

The night conceals their serried bayonets' gleam,

As cautiously they cross Tchernaya's stream ;

Yet stealthily they move as if afraid

Of entering some wily ambuscade.

Surprised to find no pickets hold the ground,[5]

They often halt to reconnoitre round.

As they make their way through the winding dell

And the dwarf-oak copse on Inkermann's fell ;

But in the lonely valley all is still,

No hostile force seems stirring on the hill ;

Not a sound is heard save a heavy tramp,

Though their columns approach the British camp.

They halt on the crest of the beetling height,

And plant their guns under cover of night ;

Then form up their ranks in battle array,

And wait for the dawn to fall on their prey.

Night wanes, and slowly breaks the dreary morn ;

Portending clouds foretell a coming storm ;

Dense vapours swiftly drift, and dark clouds fly,

At times revealing a dull leaden sky.

A drizzling rain falls heavy on the hill,[6]

The night's obscure, the distant camp is still ;[7]

And in the east is seen no cheering ray

To mark the coming of the wished-for day.

Thus, when dark clouds of dread misfortune lour,

Slowly appears to move the passing hour :

The future, like a wild tempestuous sea,

Hopeless lies hidden in uncertainty.

The breaking morn discloses to their eyes

The distant camp of those they would surprise ;

Who unprepared, and wrapped in slumber,

Look but a handful 'gainst their number.

O'erfagged with toil, and by long watching worn,

Ta'en by surprise, they must be backwards borne.—

Such was their leader's aim : his plan was wise,[8]

His troops o'er-confident already 'd gain'd the prize.

Blessed by their priests, did not the Czar decree

The fallen, Heaven—the rest, a victory ?

The royal princes, too, had joined the host,

To see fulfilled Menschikoff's proud boast,

" That with a short day's work he'd end the war,

" And crown with bays the eagles of the Czar.

" That ere the night set in, his foes should be

" All slain or ta'en, or driven to the sea."

His countless legions by a single blow,

He thought at one fell swoop, could crush—but no !

The old adage has it, "Many a slip
Oft intervenes between the cup and lip."
That leader did not know, though he was wise,
The nature of the foe he would surprise ;
He did not know that not a man would yield,
Though the last there might fall upon the field :
That every brave defender must have died,
Ere any Russian force gain that hill-side.

Exposed on all sides to the weather's brunt,[9]
Our worn-out pickets posted in the front
Of Inkermann's bleak crest, now shivering stood
O'erlooking Tchernaya's winding vale and wood.
They heed not the storm that threatening lours,
Nor the piercing blasts, nor the drizzling showers,
But pace their lone rounds on Inkermann's height,
And impatiently watch for morning's.light.

Their haggard brows, and hollow cheeks so pale,
Of fearful hardships tell a dismal tale;
Their manly forms are bent, their features wear
The deepen'd lines of suffering and of care.
Matted with mud, the tattered garments show
The weary toil those veterans undergo;
Still their proud mien, by dangers unsubdued,
Showed daring courage, dauntless fortitude.

As in the front advanced the night patrol,
They heard a distant church-bell faintly toll,[10]
Pealing throughout the night, its solemn swell
Came o'er the breeze—'twas like a funeral knell.—
Some said they heard the sullen rumbling sounds
Of rolling wheels, whilst visiting their rounds;
But all around was dark, and sable night
Concealed the valley from the watchers' sight.

They listening stood, for, borne upon the wind,

Gathering in volume strange and undefined,

Mysterious murmurs rose upon the ear

Like noise of mighty waters rushing near.

A startled owl flew hooting through the air,

. And wild dogs whining growled, couched in their lair;[11]

Strange noises too rode on the howling blast,

Though nought was seen but dense mist drifting past.

They grasped their arms, but neither breathed nor stirred,

And whisper'd low, " Was that the gale we heard?"

They strain'd their eyes, but nought discerned below,

And all was still save but the streamlet's flow:

They could not understand those sounds of fear,

And little dream'd the subtle foe lurked near.

They said " 'Tis the roar of Tchernaya's tide,

Or the moaning wind on Inkermann's side."

Yet what could have scared the dusky owl,

And caused the wild dogs to turn and growl?

c

They did not fear the swelling tempest's roar ;

'Twas the approach of man they dreaded more.

What sounds are those that issue from the glen ?

Hush!—Hark!—They strike the ear again.

Methinks I hear a heavy measured tramp,

As if some mighty host approach'd the camp.

Do ye not hear a far-off bugle sound ?

List!—Distant shots re-echo from the ground,

And shouts and cries seem rising on the ear ;

That rumbling noise is cannons' wheels, I fear.

What can it mean ?—It's surely not yet day,

Yet from our pickets come those sounds of fray :

Of a vast multitude that is the hum.

It is the enemy.   They come! they come!

Then sudden roll'd the drum its loud alarms,

And the shrill bugle rang its call "to arms;"

Each soldier started from his lowly bed,

And grasped his arms laid ready by his head;

Then o'er his cloak his pouch and belts he flung,[12]

And from his tent on towards the front he sprung.

The "assembly" sounding, warned the little band

Whom dangers threaten, where to make a stand.

From every side men poured with utmost speed,

And never had Old England's sons more need,

For dropping shots were heard along the van,

Which told the work of carnage had began.

Return'd from the trenches at break of dawn,

I lay in my tent all tired and worn,

Stretched by the side of my horse on the ground,

When on our ears burst the ominous sound.

First a strange buzz, like the noise of a crowd,

Was heard through the camp; then cries long and loud

Arose from all sides, whilst a deafening shout

Was heard in the van—"The Russians are out!"

Then bugle blasts, and rollings of the drum,

The alarm spreads; from all sides soldiers run.

Half-dressed but armed on towards the front they go,

And coolly form, prepared to meet the foe.

I grasped my sword, then for my pistols felt,

And thrust them hurriedly into my belt;

Tighten'd the girths, sprung on my eager steed,

A gallant grey of Nedjed's sacred breed,[13]

Who arched his neck, and seemed to smell afar

The tainted air, prognosticating War.

Then from his eyes flashed fire. He knew the sound:

Impatient to be off, he pawed the ground.

Ah! little thought I then, poor "Desert-born,"

That I should lose thy services that morn :

I miss thee sadly, for such friends are few,

I ne'er had one who always proved so true.

In danger's hour ne'er would thy spirit quail,

And in my need I never found thee fail :

Many a time hast thou borne me through strife,

When a swerve or a check had cost me my life.

But thine eye never blenched, thine ear never cower'd,

Though cannon have boomed and bullets have shower'd.

In the "Valley of Death," when with wild huzza

"The Light Brigade" charged the troops of the Czar,

And six hundred troopers rode against hordes,

Thy whinney was heard 'mid the clashing of swords.

Well worthy wert thou of a pacha's gift,

In beauty unsurpass'd—as lightning swift—

Of noblest blood, enduring to the last,

An Arab desert-born, of highest caste.

Little reck'd we of tempests or weather,

Hardships were nought whilst we were together;

Oft have we shared a last morsel of bread,

And slept side by side, the earth for our bed.

Thy wildest career I ever could check

By word or by sigh: my hand to thy neck

Had magical power; and if there was need

A word in thine ear would urge thee to speed.

So gentle too with all, brought up by hand

'Midst tender maidens of that Eastern land,

Thou hadst no fear of man but wert his friend—

A better one the Gods did never send.

A comrade's parting gift thou wert from one

To whom I was e'en as a father's son;

Who, as he placed thy bridle in my hand,

Said, as we stood surrounded by his band,

" All men will know *my brother* by his steed,

My friends will aid, and serve him in his need."

He, too, is gone, who was indeed a Man—

A braver never fell in battle's van.

Silistria's breach for ages will attest

How the dark Moussa sunk unto his rest.

On the crumbling walls he'd sworn to defend

That brave Arab chief met a soldier's end;

Scorning to yield, he died at his post,

When a handful of Turks resisted a host.

The Sons of the Desert revere his name,

And Araby's maidens sing of his fame;

In the tents of Sahara tears are shed

When the Santons tell of the noble dead.

END OF THE FIRST CANTO.

INKERMANN.

CANTO THE SECOND.

———◆———

THE BATTLE.

INKERMANN.

CANTO THE SECOND.

————◆◇◆————

THE BATTLE.

" By Heaven ! it is a splendid sight to see
For one who hath no friend, no brother there."

Childe Harold.

————◆◇◆————

THE hour was dark, cold, bleak, and grey,

It was not night, it seem'd not day ;

For dense mists rolling on the ground

Hid from the eye the scene around.

Still on we dashed—my gallant horse

Went bounding forward in his course,

And through the vapour made his way,

Guided by sounds of distant fray.

Like a true charger bred to war,
He smelt the battle from afar,
And onward flew, swift as a bird,
Excited by the sounds he heard.

A heavy tramp fell on the ear,
Foreboding strife and danger near,
And sounding like the distant roar
Of ocean 'gainst a rocky shore.
At times we saw dark figures loom,
And rifles flash red through the gloom,
As on the foe an outpost fired,[14]
And slowly on the camp retired;
Whilst heavy masses of the foe
Pursued like rivers' ceaseless flow.
As misty vapours lighter grew,
Clouds of skirmishers came in view,

Stealing like panthers on their prey,

All clad in cloaks of sombre grey.

A massive column too was seen

Creeping along the dark ravine,

Winding its way like serpent's trail

Towards the camp it would assail.

No drums were beat, no trumpets blown,

No sounds were heard but their tread alone,

Until their van our camp drew nigh,

When suddenly a fiendish cry

Burst from their ranks from front to rear,

Reverberating through the air,

And echo'd by the hills, they say,

It e'en reached Balaklava's bay.

The first-warned of Old England's band

By a low wall had made their stand,[15]

And with their weapons levelled low
Waited the onset of the foe.
Cold drops were bursting then, I trow,
From the young soldier's anxious brow,
As in the mist he cast a glance,
And thought of battle's desperate chance,
Yet none a sign of fear betray'd,
All there were calm and undismayed ;
Though faces might be pale and wan,
The light of battle on them shone :
Right well those men their danger knew,
But all were stanch, each heart was true,
And not a cheek amongst them blenched,
But each his rifle firmly clenched.

"They come!" one whispered 'neath his breath,
Then reigned a silence still as death ;

A minute sped, when midst the gloom

A column's head was seen to loom.

Nearer it came,—then passed the word,

The click of locks was only heard,

Each soldier then his rifle raised,

And the first dread volley blazed,

Rolling like thunder through the air,

And followed by a British cheer.

Then rose a wild despairing cry,

Then burst a shriek of agony,

It seemed as if the fiends from Hell

Had joined in that despairing yell.

That volley fearful havoc made,

And hundreds in the dust were laid ;

Still o'er their corses others tore,

To fall like those who went before :

Our soldiers battling side by side,

Against the torrent stemm'd the tide;

And oft was heard that ringing cheer

Which nerves the heart, and deadens fear.

Musketry rolled in volleys poured,

In heavy peals the cannon roared;

Through murky fogs the missiles crashed,

On every side the red flame flashed;

Huge shells were bursting all around,

And dead and dying strewed the ground;

Whilst shrieks of pain, and wild despair,

With shouts of battle rent the air.

The mist assumed a sulphurous dun

Impervious to the rising sun,

Whilst clouds of smoke rose from the fray

And hid the field from face of day;

Then floating overhead it grew

A canopy of purple hue.

As vultures swoop upon their prey,

So rushed the foe unto the fray,

And forward pressed, with the design

To seize our camp and break our line.

Their columns with tumultuous yell,

That rose above the battle's swell,

Charged 'gainst our line with heavy shock,

But broke like waves upon a rock;

Leaving their dead upon the turf,

Like foaming spray when breaks the surf.

For we received them as they came,

With withering volleys thick as rain,

Which broke the order of assault,

And forced the wavering mass to halt.

Their foremost ranks were backwards bent,

Wide gaps were in their columns rent;

Like torrent damm'd up in its course,

They stayed—'twas but to gather force;

D

Then yelling rushed to the attack,

Again our volleys hurled them back.

Once more they formed, but all in vain ;

Their ranks, encumbered by the slain,

Advanced but slowly, for their tread

Was much impeded by the dead.

A bugle sounding in our rear

Told us support was drawing near ;

Then loudly rang our wild hurrah,

Which Tchernaya's hills re-echoed far,

Swords flashed, and glistening bayonets shone,

And to the charge the line moved on.[16]

Then rose a heart-inspiring cheer

Which in itself had banished fear,

And full upon the foe we dashed,

And 'midst their ranks our bayonets clashed.

Hand to hand we showered our blows,

And loudly England's war-shout rose,

Until the foeman's fiendish cry

Was drowned by groans of agony.

Long and furious was the strife;

Our men fought recklessly for life;

Loud volleys rang, and fast and hot,

On both sides flew the ceaseless shot.

Oft foot to foot, and hand to hand,

The hostile ranks fought band to band,

Exchanging sword and bayonet thrust,

And raising up dense clouds of dust.

Reckless of odds our soldiers fought,

And fearless deeds of valour wrought,

As 'midst the hostile ranks they tore,

And thrice their numbers backwards bore.

Hard-pressed by charges oft renewed,

A panic seized the multitude;

Their wavering ranks could not sustain.
They broke and scattered o'er the plain.

Their officers, when they beheld
Their host thus humbled and repell'd.
Of their own lives but little recked,
If that their fall our onset checked.
Striving the dire retreat to stay,
They forced their men to face the fray ;
E'en struck the flying with the sword,
But nought could stop the routed horde.
Who fled in terror from our force.
Long lanes of dead marking their course.

Whilst the foe were wildly flying.
We advanced o'er dead and dying.

And in pursuit fast onward pressed

To the brow of Inkermann's crest;

When suddenly the air was rent

And darkened grew the firmament;

Like thunder rolled artillery's war,

For ninety guns upon us bore.

Huge shells were hurtling all around,

Whilst shot and grape ploughed up the ground,

Covering well the foe's retreat,

And saving them from dire defeat:

For our few guns could scarce oppose

The heavier pieces of the foe's,

Until two siege-guns from the rear

Were brought upon their front to bear;

And gained us respite to draw breath,

By their winged messengers of death.

Just then we heard a thrilling cheer,

Rolling along from front to rear,

And reining up his panting steed

Reeking with foam, from reckless speed,

The leader of our host drew nigh,

And the whole line took up the cry.

" I thank ye all, my men," he said,

Uncovering his stately head,

And bowing to his charger's mane,

He cantered towards the front again.

Right noble was Lord Raglan's mien ;

Many the red field he had seen,

For he had fought on Belgium's plain,

And in the bloody wars of Spain,

When the great Duke with iron hand

Raised his standard in that land,

And made the British soldier's name

Ring through the world for deeds of fame,

Gaining for Britain and her crown
Unfading laurels and renown,
Such as no chief had ever won
Before the days of Wellington.
Inured to strife, our leader's eye
Betokened innate bravery,
Such as no peril e'er could shake
Or dire adversity e'er break.
In duty firm, his heart was kind,
His manly face portrayed his mind,
And all the feelings of his breast
Were in his countenance expressed.
He knew the Island-soldiers' worth,
The best and bravest on the earth ;
And loved by them, he had the power
To cheer their hearts in danger's hour.

Still sullenly the cannon's boom
Was heard resounding through the gloom,
And now again the foe's array
Was seen advancing to the fray.

On the crest of Inkermann's height,
In an angle towards the right,
A sand-bag battery had been plann'd
Tchernaya's valley to command.
Unfinished still, no guns were laid [17]
That might a foe's advance have stay'd;
But the flower of Britain's host,
The Royal Guards, then held the post.
Their " thin red line " dare never yield
Though all might fall upon the field,
And George of Cambridge held command,
A worthy chief of such a band.

A warning blast our bugles blew ;

From rank to rank a whisper flew

" That foes in force assailed the height,

Hidden by vapour from our sight."

A strange hum rising from the ground

Warned us of dangers gathering round,

Still the thick mist their force concealed,

Until a musket's flash revealed

A mighty horde, which, close at hand,

Seemed to surround our little band.

On every side their helmets glanced,

Wave upon wave of men advanced,

And with a wild exulting shout,

Assailed in thousands the redoubt.

Then long and loud our thunders roared,

Sharp volleys in the mass were poured ;

Their van fell lifeless on the plain,

Still others took the lead again,

And clambering over corses piled,

Came on, with shrieks and yells as wild,

As if from hell the fiends had broke,

And hovered round us in the smoke.

Death stayed, but could not stop their course;

They poured in overwhelming force,[18]

And closing round upon our flanks

Bore down against our weakened ranks,

Who faint, and breathless, soil'd with blood,

For hours the fearful odds withstood.

Four times before our charge they broke,

Four times they rallied in the smoke;

Though hundreds fell still hosts remained

Who rushing on the fight maintained.

As hungry wolves enclose their prey,

The Russians held the Guards at bay,

Who unsubdued, fought back to back,

Exposed on all sides to attack.

There seemed no prospect of escape,

Death hovered round in every shape ;

No aid could come, their doom seemed sealed,

Still undismayed, they held the field,

And closing up, renewed the fight

For Honour and Old England's right.

From the dense horde was heard afar

A sullen howl, their cry of war,

To which our men with cheers replied,

And closing shoulder side by side,

With their bayonets levell'd low,

Burst like a whirlwind on the foe :

Then rose the steel's loud ringing clash,

Then gleamed the musket's deadly flash,

Then burst strange cries of wild despair,

Then rang a cheer which rent the air.

Nought could the fearful onset stay,

On every side the foe gave way :

Their heavy force was backwards bent,

And the huge mass in twain was rent.

Right gallantly those Guardsmen fought,

And fearful deeds of valour wrought,

Holding their own against the mass,

Who strove in vain our line to pass.

Though oft repulsed, the Russians still

Strove to regain the blood-stained hill;

And hordes advanced against our right

Up a ravine most hid from sight.

Cathcart, though with inferior force,

Attacked this column in its course,

Poured in its ranks a heavy fire,

And forced it broken to retire ;

When in his rear, crowning the height,

Other battalions came in sight ;

And on all sides, above, below,

Appeared dense masses of the foe.

Firm and unyielding, as a rock

Sustains the heaving billow's shock,

Our men maintained the fearful strife,

And neither gave nor asked for life.

Though in a narrow ring beset,

Each fresh attack was boldly met ;

As one man fell, his comrades closed,

And still a sturdy front opposed.

At last the ammunition failed,

And front and rear were both assailed ;

This was the crisis of the fray :
Our men like lions stood at bay,
Holding their own, oft back to back,
Exposed on all sides to attack.
None sued for quarter—it were vain.
We saw our helpless comrades slain,
Slain in cold blood, as on the ground
They fell disabled from a wound.

Conspicuous 'mid that dreadful scene,
By his cool air and dauntless mien,
The gallant Cathcart cheer'd his men,
And led them to the charge again.
Where the danger threatened worst,
There was our leader ever first ;
As if he bore a charmed life,
And revelled fearless 'mid the strife.

" Give them the steel, my lads!" he cried,

The men with hearty cheers replied,

And ere the red-flam'd volley flashed,

Amid their ranks our bayonets crashed.

Half blinded by the blaze and smoke,

Through their serried ranks we broke ;

Then smothered shots and steel's loud clang,

'Mid groans and shrieks of anguish rang ;

On every side was heard the cry

Of those who kill, of those who die ;

And hideous yells of wild despair,

With cheers of triumph rent the air.

As through the foe a path we hew'd,

Our course with lanes of dead lay strew'd,

And e'en the very ground we trod

Was slippery with human blood.

Then was the gallant Cathcart slain—

A musket bullet pierced his brain,

And ere an eye could mark the wound
Both horse and man rolled on the ground.
There bravely fighting by his side,
The stalwart Seymour nobly died,
And Dowling, Wynn, and many more
With their chief lay stretched in gore.
Breathless and faint, our shattered ranks
At last regained the sloping banks,
And there re-formed their lessened front,
Prepared again for battle's brunt.

Stung with discomfiture and rage,
The foe pressed on to re-engage
Our little band, who pant for breath,
But still maintain the strife of death ;
When a fresh column from the right,
Moved quickly forward to the fight,

And poured a volley in the foe,

Who writhed from this unlooked-for blow.

It was the French ! just come in time,

To aid our sadly-weaken'd line,

Which in the front, from early morn,

Had all the brunt of battle borne ;

And who though faint from constant fight,

Still held their own upon the height.

As they dashed up, we gave a cheer,

And joined them in their bold career :

" Vive l'Empereur !" was now the cry

As to the charge his children fly,

And British cheers as we advance

Mingle with shouts of " Vive la France !"

Again upon the foe we dash'd,

Again amid their ranks we crash'd,

Again our thunders loudly roar'd,

Again our deadly volleys pour'd,

Again we charged home through the smoke,

Again their massive columns broke,

Again their deafening cannon fired,

Again repulsed the foe retired ;

Again was heard Old England's cry,

As we dashed on to victory ;

Again was heard the Frenchman's shout.

As they rush'd forward in pursuit,

And, by the gallant Bosquet led,

Fast follow'd up the foe who fled.

Fearful the carnage that ensued,

As the Allies the foes pursued,

For thousands fell upon the plain,

Who never more arose again.

 END OF THE SECOND CANTO.

INKERMANN.

CANTO THE THIRD.

— · ◦◆ —

THE FIELD OF BATTLE.

INKERMANN.

CANTO THE THIRD.

———◆◆———

THE FIELD OF BATTLE.

" There is something of pride in the perilous hour,
    Whate'er be the shape in which death may lour ;
    For Fame is there to say who bleeds,
    And Honour's eye on daring deeds !
    But when all is past, it is humbling to tread
    O'er the weltering field of the tombless dead,
    And see worms of the earth, and fowls of the air,
    Beasts of the forest, all gathering there ;
    All regarding man as their prey,
    All rejoicing in his decay."

The Siege of Corinth.

———◆◆———

AT last the bloody field was won,

The sword was sheathed, its task was done.

The foe repulsed, attacked no more,

Though still we heard their cannon roar.

Many a youth whose hopes beat high,

Scarce dreaming he could ever die,

In early morn brim-full of mirth,

At eve lay cold upon the earth.

A loathsome mass, Red, Blue, and Grey,

A ghastly pile of mangled clay,

Marks where our friends and foes pell-mell,

Heaped on each other fighting fell.

There British, French, and Russians sleep,

Stretched side by side in slumber deep,

Ne'er to wake till the trumpet's bray

Shall sound upon the Judgment-day:

When earth shall hear the summons dread,

And ocean from her rocky bed,

Shall yield up those whose unknown graves

Are on the shore or 'neath the waves.

Many a hard-fought day I've seen,

On battle's field I'd often been,

But ne'er beheld so sad a sight

As that hill-side after the fight;

For dead and wounded strewed the plain,

The living oft beneath the slain.

Thousands, in their warm blood lying,

Parched by thirst were hopeless dying;

Some in agony passed away,

Calling on friends, trying to pray;

Some as they yielded up their life,

Breathed name of mother or of wife,

And gazed around with vacant stare,

Seeking for those they found not there.

Some mad with fever's thirst, and pain,

Wandered delirious o'er the plain,

Until they reached the streamlet's side,

There drank their fill, lay down and died.

Some rising from the cold damp ground

Made vain attempts to stanch their wound,

Dabbling their hands in crimson stains,

As the life's stream ebb'd from their veins.

Some proudly smiled in their last breath,

Some scowled in anger e'en in death;

Some seemed to die without a care,

Whilst others raving tore their hair;

Some looked around in wild amaze,

And wandering talked of bygone days;

Some called on God in their despair,

Or tried to recollect a prayer.

In groups along the rugged crest

Grim marksmen lay with lips comprest,

Stern-knitted brows, and rifle clenched,

Although the face in death was blenched.

Some there were still upon their knees,

Couching behind the stunted trees,

As if they still maintain'd the strife,

And that their limbs were full of life.

One held a foe within his grasp,

And still maintained his dying clasp,

Whilst firmly clenched in his right hand

And raised to strike, was the red brand;

But death-shots rang, ere the blow sped,

And both antagonists were dead,

Though save a strange, cold, vacant stare,

No sign announced the spoiler there.

Crushed underneath a lifeless horse

Lay in the dust a mangled corse,

Which still instinctively retained

A broken rein and sword blood-stained.

Whilst by its side a wounded hound

Couched whimpering upon the ground,

As if he could not understand

Why aid came not from that cold hand:

As if to claim one last caress,

He licked the cheek, and pulled the dress,

But finding all his efforts vain,

With whining cry and look of pain,

He gazed, as if he seemed to trace

The change upon his master's face,

And then, as if all hope had fled,

Gave one long howl, and fell back dead.

The ground bore marks of bloody fray,

And broken swords and helmets lay

Strewed o'er the field with shot and grape,

And arms of every kind and shape.

Where corses piled marked fiercest strife,

Though wounded, one gave signs of life,

In whose pale features I could trace

The semblance of an old friend's face,

Whom I had known in days gone by,

When life was new, and hopes were high.

Could it be he?—I breathed his name,

A wild start shook his troubled frame;

He knew my voice, and shook his head,

"The game is up," he faintly said.

Then rising with convulsive throe,

He cast a last look towards the foe,

Wiped from his brow death's clammy dew,

Which rolling down obscured his view,

And strained his eyes to watch the fray,

E'en though his life's blood ebbed away.

Long thus he gazed, but did not speak,

Though transient glows diffused his cheek;

His kindling eyes flashed wildly bright,

Shining with strange, unearthly light,

And a proud melancholy smile
Played o'er his features for a while,
Then from his lips burst forth a cry,
" Hurrah!   We've won the victory!"

His lip then quivered, and his breast
Heaved with convulsive pangs oppress'd ;
His fading eyes were upwards cast,
The shades of death were gathering fast ;
He felt his youthful strength fast sink,
He felt the sod his life-blood drink ;
He saw it welling from his wound,
And streaming down upon the ground.
He laid him down without a sigh,
He knew his hour had come to die ;
He reck'd not of the life he gave,
He reck'd not of his early grave,

He reck'd not that his hour was come.

He knew the bloody field was won :

He knew that he had bravely fought,

And with his blood success was bought ;

E'en though he felt his end was nigh,

He strove to check a rising sigh,

For thoughts, " What friends at home would say,"

Flash'd o'er his mind like a bright ray

Through gloomy skies, when dark clouds lour,

Cheering his soul in that sad hour.

Yet grief for loved ones left behind

Oppress'd that gallant soldier's mind ;

When he thought of home, far away,

And of his mother, old and grey ;

Of the dear girl he'd see no more,

'Twas then his sinking heart felt sore.

Who now shall comfort, dry their tears ?

Who now support her failing years ?

Now she is friendless, childless, lone,

He was her first, her only one.

He turned away and heaved a sigh,

A tear was bursting from his eye ;

" Tell them—you know," he feebly said,

To hide his grief he turned his head,

And flung his arms around my neck,

Sobbing as if his heart would break.

His pallid cheek my shoulder pressed,

His head drooped low upon my breast,

Fierce spasms wrung his clammy brow,

He gasped for breath, then murmuring low,

" Tell her," he said, with half-drawn sigh,

" 'Twas ever thus I wished to die."

He closed his eyes, and gently sighed,

To breathe a prayer at times he tried;

But now his voice began to fail,

His look was fixed, his lips were pale;

From loss of blood he grew more weak

Until at last he scarce could speak;

Yet, reckless of his dying pain,

He took my hand in his again,

And as it lay within his clasped,

I felt it gently once more grasped,

Whilst smothering a broken sigh,

He whispered, " Hal, old friend, good-bye !"

Then came the heavy hand of death,

He drew convulsively his breath;

And gasping from his mouth black gore,

Drew one long sigh, and all was o'er.

NIGHT AFTER THE BATTLE.

———◦◦◦———

The night now gathers, all around is still,

Save a low murmur from Tchernaya's rill,

Whose rippling waves bright in the moonlight gleam,

As towards the sea onwards flows the stream ;

At times is heard the wild-dog's doleful howl,

Or the loud hooting of the horned night owl

Above the weird moan of dark Euxine's surge,

Which strikes on the ear like a slow sad dirge.

The silvery moon her watch is keeping

O'er the battle-field, where calmly sleeping

Beneath the pale rays of her gentle light,

Now rest side by side the fallen in fight ;

The locks of the dead are stirred by the breeze
That sweeps o'er the plain and sighs through the trees.
There mangled they lie on the cold damp earth,
Far, far away from the land of their birth.

Go, Zephyr, and breathe this sad tale of death
In our English homes with thy softest breath;
Break to our kindred the friends they have lost,
And tell them the price that Inkermann cost.
Tell the aged sire, who has lost his son,
"That the foe have fled, that the fight was won,
"That his noble boy in the van was slain,"
'Twill comfort his heart and deaden the pain:
And to the mother whose sole earthly pride
Was he who lies still on that bleak hill-side;
Console with thoughts that he's but gone before,
To a land where they'll meet to part no more.

F

But to she who kneels with hands up clasped,

Breathing a prayer for him who passed

Like a flower away, cut off in his prime,

Ye cannot console, 'tis the work of time.

Break the news gently, or sorrow may kill,

And life pass away in cry wild and shrill;

Keen anguish may burst the chords of the heart:

The tale must be told, may God ease the smart!

Go breathe in the ear of the Island's Queen

Of victory won, of sights thou hast seen.

Tell her, " Her children have conquered again,

That Honours are won, though few now remain ;"

Say " That the remnant would gladly lay down

Their lives in her service, to gain her renown."

That duty but points the path they would go.

Honour to Britain, and death to her foe.

Scutari Hospital.

END OF THE THIRD AND LAST CANTO.

NOTES TO INKERMANN.

INKERMANN.

Note 1. Page 4.

Sevastopol from Cathcart's Hill.

The chain of Russian sentries who were posted along the most advanced front of the ramparts were in the habit of uttering loud cries every quarter of an hour, which passed along the whole line, each sentry taking it up in his turn. Thus the men on out-post duty were always kept on the alert, and if any of them slept on their post, or deserted to the enemy, it was soon discovered.

Note 2. Page 4.

No one who bore a part in this campaign can forget the peculiarly mournful sounds of the wind as it rushed howling through the steep ravines and gorges amid the bleak hills and cliffs of that iron-bound coast. Over and over again, especially whilst on duty in the still night, do I remember it appearing to sound, like far-off music, slow, sad, and melancholy.

Note 3. Page 5.

The Moaning of the Wind.

In Circassia, when the inhabitants hear the wind moaning among the mountains of the Caucasus, they say that " it is the voices of the

dead, in the land of spirits," and some who profess the occult science
pretend to interpret its meaning. This strange weird-like music has
a peculiar effect even upon animals. I remember, whilst travelling
below the spurs of Mount Elburz, coming across a pack of seven
wolves who were sitting on their haunches in a semicircle, making
the most extraordinary noises, as if they were trying to imitate the
sound of the wind, which at the time was moaning wildly amongst
the mountains. They were so much absorbed in their demon-like
chorus, that they did not notice our approach, and we watched them
for some time. My companions said that " the wolves were talking to
the spirits of their ancestors, whose voices issued from their abode
above the endless snow wastes on the mountain."

Note 4.   Page 11.

The Gathering.

The Russian advance was made in the greatest silence, and every
precaution taken to insure success.

One of their columns crossed the river Tchernaya at the head of
the harbour by the bridge, marching along the road above the ravine
of the quarries. A *second* issued from the town, which was intended
to cut off our force from the assistance of the French. A *third* crossed
the Tchernaya by the bridge on the Inkermann road, and gaining the
heights, attacked the camp of our second division. A *fourth* attack
was intended to have been made by Liprandi's force (which con-
sisted of thirty-two squadrons of regular cavalry and Cossacks, with
several batteries of artillery and some infantry) in order to threaten
Balaklava, and hold in check both General Bosquet's and Sir Colin
Campbell's force; but he only made a slight demonstration, and
General Bosquet's division came to our assistance about four hours
and a half after the battle had begun. A *fifth* attacking column fell

upon the extreme left of the French trenches by the Quarantine Fort, but was repulsed with great loss by General Lourmelle, who was killed close to the enemy's works.

A telegraph had been erected on the heights of Inkermann, to signalise to the garrison of Sevastopol the moment of the attack of the Russian army on our camp, so that at the same time they might make two sorties on different parts of our trenches.—*My Log.*

Note 5. Page 12.

The Midnight March.

The enemy were much surprised, when they advanced to attack our position, to find that *we had no outposts in the valley of the Tchernaya,* for they imagined we should have had heavy batteries on the heights commanding the bridge and valley below. Sir De Lacy Evans, with the experience of an old soldier, had frequently pointed out the insecurity of the undefended flanks of our position, but his wise warnings were not attended to. Under cover of the darkness of the morning, the enemy dragged up several pieces of heavy artillery, and placed them in position ready to open fire on our camp at daybreak.

Note 6. Page 13.

Daybreak.

The morning of the battle was extremely dark; several drizzling showers had fallen during the night, and just before dawn a heavy mist hung on the ground, and settled on the heights, and in the valley of Inkermann.

Note 7. Page 13.

In the British camp all appeared quiet. There all was security and repose; and little did our slumbering troops imagine that a subtle and indefatigable enemy had advanced huge masses of men under cover of powerful artillery to a very formidable position, and were only waiting for the first glimpse of daylight, and the dispersion of the fogs, to fall upon their unsuspecting prey.

Note 8. Page 14.

The Vaunt.

"The Russian general knew the immense advantages under which he fought. In the first place, he had a very great superiority in numbers; had an overpowering artillery of much larger calibre than ours; his men were well fed, sheltered from the weather, and full of confidence. Besides which, they were incited by their priests, and promised success, fighting under the eyes of the sons of the Czar, whom they are taught to consider the delegate of God. On the other hand, he knew that our army was far too small to operate with any chance of success; that our men were worn out by constant exposure, and continual hard work; that they sustained the most unheard-of hardships, often wanting even a bare sufficiency of food. When all the advantages the enemy possessed over the Allies are considered, the Russian general's boast cannot be wondered at, for victory must have appeared but as a natural consequence to a leader who did not know the indomitable, sterling courage of the British soldier, and who had not then experienced the bitter defeat of an Inkermann."—*My Log.*

Note 9. Page 15.

The Outlying Picket.

" The pickets and outlying posts were thoroughly saturated, and
their arms wet, despite their precautions; and it is scarcely to be
wondered at if there were some of them not quite so alert as sentries
should be in face of an enemy, for it must be remembered that our
small army was almost worn out by incessant labour, and that even
the sentries on picket were frequently men who had had but a short
respite from work in the trenches or regimental duty.   Besides, on the
morn of Inkermann the fog and vapours of drifting rain were so thick
that one could hardly see two yards before him."—*Press.*

Note 10. Page 16.

The Warning.

" At four o'clock the bells of the churches of Sevastopol were
heard ringing drearily through the cold night-air ; but the occurrence
had been so usual that it excited no particular attention.   During the
night, however, a sharp-eared sergeant on an outlying picket of the
Light Division heard the sound of wheels in the valley below as
though they were approaching the position up the hill.   He reported
the circumstance to Major Bunbury; but it was supposed that the
sound arose from ammunition waggons or arabas going into Sevastopol
by the Inkermann road.   No one suspected for a moment that
enormous masses of Russians were creeping up the rugged sides of
the heights over the valley of Inkermann on the undefended flank of
the Second Division."—*Russell.*

Note 11. Page 17.

" A very large kind of sheep-dog is common in this part of the Crimea, and the inhabitants having fled, these guardians of the fold keep together in troops, living in holes and caves, and feeding on the carcasses of the horses and other dead bodies. Some have become perfectly wild, and, from their gaunt appearance and habits, have been mistaken for wolves. A large troop of upwards of twenty held possession of the hardly-contested ground between our advanced trenches and the fortifications of the town, notwithstanding the fearful cross-fire of shot, shell, grape, and musketry that continually swept over it. These dogs were often hunted by the mounted officers of the allied armies. I have seen upwards of two hundred at a meet near Karani, from grave generals to jolly subalterns."—*My Log.*

Note 12. Page 19.

The Assembly.

The battle of Inkermann was fought by the British army in their cloaks, which is a very unusual costume for them in action, full dress being generally worn. The French are in the habit of dressing unusually smart when they expect a general action. My friend, the late Lieut.-Col. Magnan, of the État Major-General, had reserved a new tunic and epaulettes, with a pair of Piver's white kid gloves expressly for the assault of Sevastopol, where he fell mortally wounded inside the Malakoff. How does this contrast with the Russian habit of officers of the highest rank wearing the same costume as that of the private soldier ? It certainly has one good effect, as it prevents the officers from being picked off.

Note 13.   Page 20.

The Arab Charger.

The bones of my poor horse, "Desert-born," whitened on the hillside of Inkermann, where he was killed by a shell, and his master severely wounded. He was a parting present from the celebrated Arab chief, Moussa Pacha, who was killed on the ramparts of Silistria, and was a perfect specimen of the pure Nedjed Arab. In the beginning of the campaign, I always *turned in* dressed, so as to be ready for service at a moment's notice. One side of my tent I had dug out to the depth of nearly three feet, and this part was occupied by my favourite charger. The nights were often bitterly cold; we were not overburdened with clothes; fuel was scarce, and not to be had without much trouble, so I found keeping my horse in my tent answered a double purpose—it preserved him from the weather, and served to keep me warm. Two other companions also shared my tent, for in a beautiful deserted villa on the Balbec I found a brace of Russian pointers, chained up and nearly famished, which I appropriated, and they used to sleep coiled up at my feet, and served as an extra blanket. Often in the morning, when I awoke, I have found my horse with his head stretched as far as he could reach over the heap of dry leaves that formed my bed, and his beautiful gazelle-like eyes fixed on my face; and sometimes in the night I would feel him "*mouthing*" my hand in the most gentle manner, as if to make sure that I was near him. He had been my constant companion during several months' active service on the Danube, and we fully understood each other. His affectionate disposition and extraordinary sagacity had quite endeared him to me, and when he was killed I felt as if I had lost a well-loved friend.

The Arabian horse, the sire and progenitor of the English racehorse, has been the subject of many lengthy papers; but I have not read one account that tallies with that of the Bedouins, who say that there are five breeds among the "ussal khomsee," or horses of true family, *i.e.*, thorough-breds, and that they are descended from the five sacred mares of Mahomet, named Rabdha, Noama, Wajza, Sabha, and Heyma, giving names to the following distinct breeds—the Taueyse, Manekye, Keheyl, Saklawye, and Dujlfe. Nedjed signifies, in Arabic, high or table-land, in contradistinction to Telema, or the plains, and horses of this caste are considered the best blood of Arabia. In the desert a pedigree is never given or asked for, every Arab knowing the genealogy of another's mare, without the aid of a stud book; but for mercantile purposes, and especially in the case of colts, a properly-attested pedigree is enclosed in a piece of leather and fastened round the horse's neck.

The Mussulman does everything in a different way to a European : on entering the house, he takes off his shoes, we our hats; he shaves his head, we our beards; he values a mare, we a horse; with him the produce takes rank from the dam, with us the sire gives nobility. An Arab might sell a horse of the best breed, but a mare—never; she must be taken from him by force; and, in consequence of this, most famous mares are the property of three or four persons : as by this means the thief will have to evade three or four pairs of eyes, or the spoiler vanquish three or four individuals before the prize can be gained.

The love the Arabs bear to their mares is exemplified by an anecdote which was told me by the celebrated chieftain, Mahomet Ben Abdullah, better known as Bou Maza (the son of the Goat), whose daring exploits and hair-breadth escapes, in his predatory expeditions against the French, have caused his name to become famous in song among the santons of the desert. One of the tribes of the Djdjhura mountains possessed a coal-black mare of the pure Nedjed breed, which in the desert was of untold value, for her fame had gone forth far and wide, and the tribes were wont to swear by her fleetness and endurance. Bou Maza, then a young man, determined to possess her either by fair or foul means, and offered the whole of his wealth in exchange—viz., several tents and slaves, forty camels, sixteen other horses, and even his two wives; but nothing would induce Ben Alli the Sheik (who was the principal owner) to part with her. Bou Maza, who was on friendly terms with the Djiljhura tribes, then determined to obtain her by stealth; but this was a difficult operation, as there were always people watching night and day. After many days' consideration, and (as he told me) severe praying to Allah to sharpen his wits, he fixed upon a plan, and forthwith proceeded to execute it. He cut himself with a knife about the face and chest, and wounded his horse; and one day about noon claimed the protection of Ben Alli the Sheik, stating that he had been attacked by some Arabs of a neighbouring tribe, with whom there was a blood feud, who were lurking about in the vicinity. In the desert, "the friends of our friends are our friends, and the enemies of our friends are also our enemies," so the Sheik sent out his young men to retaliate, and follow up the supposed aggressors, whilst he and the Hakeem of the tribe bound up the wounds and attended on Bou Maza, who pretending to be in a dying state, begged that they would carry him out to a sward where the cattle of the tribe were grazing, so that he might turn his face towards the sacred city, and perform his devotions. His wish was complied with, and he soon had the gratification of beholding this famous mare, cropping the stunted herbage a short distance from the clump of date-trees, under the shade of which he was lying. She was strictly watched by two of the tribe, who for two hours hardly ever seemed to take their eyes off her, and Bou Maza began to think that the young men would return before his undertaking could be accomplished; he therefore uttered a loud cry as if in agony, which brought the watchers to his side, and selecting his opportunity, he plunged a knife, which he had concealed under his haic (dress), in their breasts, killing them ere they could utter a cry; and flinging his burnouse over their bodies, unfastened the tether which hobbled the mare's fore feet, and springing on her back, was far away in the desert before the theft was discovered. When it was found out, the Sheik, Ben Alli, whose son was one of the slain, and all the men of the tribe set off in pursuit, and after a chase of three days almost surprised him, near one of those immense salt marshes which are so numerous in Algeria, in a place where there was no means of escape, but across this dangerous ground; and Bou Maza was about to attempt it when the Sheik, Ben Alli, seeing the ignominious fate which awaited his beloved mare, forgot his revenge for the loss of his son, and begged him to forbear, giving his sacred pledge that his tribe should not molest him, or continue the pursuit for three days should he do so, preferring to run the chance of regaining her another time to seeing her perish before his eyes. Bou Maza accepted the pledge and got away. Another time he was hard run by the same tribe, and the Sheik, who headed the pursuing party, being mounted upon the own brother of the mare, finding he was not gaining ground, desisted from the chase, and cried out for him to stop and not fatigue the mare to save his wretched life, and bidding him drink the water with which her feet was washed, in token of his being indebted to her for his preservation. The abduction of this celebrated mare gave rise to a feud between the tribes in which several hundred Arabs lost their lives; and she participated in most of Bou Maza's daring exploits which made his name so terrible to those tribes who had submitted to the French.

In breeding, the Arabs pay much more attention to the caste and blood of the dam than to the sire, whereas we are too prone to expect good produce from any kind of a mare provided the horse is a thorough-bred, which is a great mistake. I believe the finest breed of horses in the world would be produced by coupling our thorough-bred English mares with Arab stallions of pure blood, as what we might lose in size we should gain in endurance.

Note 14.   Page 28.

The Outposts driven in.

The pickets of the second division were the first with whom the enemy came in contact; and they had hardly made out the grey coats of the attacking force through the dense fog that hung on the ground, when they were obliged to retire from a sharp close fire of musketry, and were driven up the brow of the hill, contesting every step, and keeping up a brisk fire on the assailants as long as they had a round of ammunition in their pouches.

"It soon became evident that the enemy, under cover of a vast cloud of skirmishers, supported by dense columns of infantry, and numerous batteries of artillery, having gained the heights during the night, was advancing in force against our position; and had during the foggy morning placed several heavy guns in position on the high ground to the left and front of the second division."—LORD RAGLAN's *Despatch.*

Note 15.   Page 29.

The First Stand.

A low stone wall about four feet high runs along the outside of the camp of the second division, about fifty paces from the tents of the 30th and 55th regiments. It was here that the first stand was made; and the numerous marks (still to be seen) of shot, shell, grape, and musketry, show how fearful was the struggle between the first warned and the Russian van   The firing of the retreating pickets had spread an alarm through the camp of the second division, and both men and officers of the different regiments rushed up, many half-dressed, with their arms in their hands. It was an anxious moment, and men looked askingly at each other, as if they wondered what the distant hum and sounds of strife might portend. In the front, towards the slope of the hill every now and again sharp cracks of the rifle were heard, followed by the roll of musketry. Then red flashes were seen through the dense fog which hung on the ground, and the heavy measured tramp of masses of men was now distinctly heard approaching. I cantered forward to reconnoitre, and met two wounded men coming towards the camp, who said that the whole Russian army was close at hand. Almost immediately afterwards our retreating pickets came in view, still keeping up a straggling fire on the advancing foe, who replied by heavy volleys. At this moment Sir William Codrington (then commanding a brigade of the Light Division) rode hurriedly by, and as bullets were whistling about rather sharply, and I did not see any object to be gained by remaining with the retiring pickets, I returned towards the camp, and found that about two thousand men of different regiments of the second division, chiefly the 30th, 55th, 41st, 47th, 49th, and 95th, were formed in line behind the stone wall previously alluded to, which number was increased by small parties who ran up from all directions in companies, tens, and even single men. Regiments had but little time to form, for the heavy tread of the enemy was heard as they approached nearer and nearer, driving back our outposts, who fell in with our line. Then a rattling of arms was heard, and almost immediately clouds of dusky figures appeared looming largely through the fog, whose long grey coats and flat caps left us no doubt as to whom they were. Through breaks in the drifting vapour, behind these swarms of skirmishers we could perceive the head of an immense column closely following in steady and compact order. A deadly silence reigned; men peered through the gloom at the advancing foe, then looked at each other. Bloodless lips and pale faces might have been seen, for the men were worn with toil, constant exposure, and hardships dreadful even to relate, and their haggard, meagre, and pinched-up features showed that they were suffering from an insufficiency of food; still there was an air of cool determination and unflinching fearless bravery portrayed on every countenance, that betokened the high bearing of the British soldier; and notwithstanding the fearful array against us, no fears were entertained for a moment as to the ultimate success of the day. Our men had a confidence and reliance in each other that was not to be shaken or daunted even by the overpowering odds displayed against them. Not a word was spoken nor a sound heard except the clicking of locks as the men raised the hammers of their rifles, no unsteadiness or wavering was to be seen along 'that thin red line.' "Aim low " was some old soldier's caution; and simultaneously a long withering volley was poured into the adverse ranks, and a fearful yell, an agonising shriek of despair followed the report. Some few of the Russian skirmishers, hidden by the smoke, managed to get into our line, but they were almost immediately bayoneted or shot down.

The loud yell of the enemy was taken up by the whole depth of the column, and they returned an ill-directed volley which did not do us much damage. Our Minie rifles kept up a long rolling fire on their dense masses, sweeping down the head of their column, and preventing the possibility of any formation. Then was seen the great superiority of the Minie rifle, for our murderous fire cleft huge gaps to the very centre of their leading battalions, sweeping down whole files and ranks entire, and many a soldier blessed the Minister of War (the Duke of Newcastle) for his wise policy in arming the troops with this weapon. The carnage was fearful; the enemy's immense masses of men were obliged to halt and move away the heaps of corpses that impeded their advance, and they could not deploy, as the whole front was encumbered by the dead.

The column appeared to reel and waver about like a huge snake writhing in its death agony; still our men steadily kept up their fearful fire, which was but ill returned. Our loss was trifling compared to theirs, for the effect of our concentrated fire can hardly be imagined. The enemy's artillery played unceasingly on our position; shot, shell, grape, and canister flew about in all directions, but luckily for us, the same fog which had obscured the advance of the enemy also prevented them from getting our range accurately, though we afterwards suffered much during the intervals between their successive attacks.—*My Log.*

Note 16.   Page 34.

The First Charge of the Second Division.

It is not possible to imagine a more exciting scene than a charge of British troops, when with a loud shrill ringing cheer, which almost drowns the rolling of drums and blasts of bugles, each man feeling confident of success lowers his bayonet and throws himself upon the foe. At such a moment all thoughts of personal danger vanish, and even the raw unfledged recruit just taken from his mother's hearth proves himself a hero, and feels and acts as if the turning-point of the day depended upon his own individual exertions. Then it is that the British soldier shows himself to be of sterling metal, and shines in a light incontestably superior to that of any other nation. His extreme coolness, combined with his sturdy bull-dog courage, his superior strength, weight, and size, and his knowledge of his own power, give him great advantages in the *mêlée*, whilst his unflinching loyalty to his Queen, his innate love of country, and a patriotism in him more instinct than inculcated animates him to deeds of daring in the field, and in the hour of need enables him to sustain the fearful privations and hardships which at times it is his lot to undergo. Inkermann, besides adding another glorious name to the annals of Old England, has shown that British soldiers have not degenerated; and the day will come when the merits of those who fought that day will be better appreciated, and their services more liberally rewarded. The old race of gallant veterans who fought and conquered under the great Duke are passing away; another generation has succeeded them, and in time to come, when ours shall be as the days of old, the few survivors of that desperate fight will be held of much account;

and when future wars shall threaten, his counsel will be taken, and they will say " Hear the old man ; he fought at Inkermann."—*My Log.*

Note 17. Page 40.

The Sand-bag Battery.

The work was a simple epaulement, with embrasures for guns made of fascines and sandbags ; but it was not armed, as from its exposed and isolated position cannon left in it would only have invited capture. It was here that the brigade of Guards suffered so severely.

Note 18. Page 42.

The Guards at Bay.

" The enemy, though they frequently advanced to the charge with great determination, uttering loud yells and shouts, could not successfully stand against us when it came to a struggle with the bayonet. The British soldier is unequalled when the contest comes to such close quarters that he can feel his adversary's breath, and cold steel has to decide the affair; for over and over again that day were large masses of the enemy driven back and repulsed by very inferior numbers of our men with the bayonet alone, and hand-to-hand combats were to be seen in breaks of the fog on every side."—*My Log.*

THE END OF NOTES.

MISCELLANEOUS POEMS AND SONGS.

THE BASHI-BAZOUK.

"Simple are thy ways, Numidia!
Many years have fail'd to change
The free customs of thy people,
Tameless, resolute, and strange!
Thus it was that Ishmael wander'd
O'er Arabia's sandy lea;
Thus it was when Islam triumph'd,
And in after days shall be."—*Viscount Maidstone.*

———◦◦———

THE Bashi-Bazouks have come from afar,

Lured by the prospect of plunder and war

From Anadol's hills to the Danube's banks,

All the wild spirits have joined the ranks,

   To wage war 'gainst the Giaour.

To aid the Sultan in his hour of need,

The Santon has mounted his Nedjed steed ;

Throughout all Islam a whisper has pass'd,

And rous'd up her sons, like a trumpet's blast,

      At night when the foe is nigh.

Bands of fierce horsemen, from regions afar,

Come, guiding their course by the Northern star ;

And the clanging cymbal and Tartar drum

Are heard in the plain as the horde moves on

      To join the Sultan's host

Swarthy Arabs have left their desert home

With the wily Kurd and Turk to roam ;

Whilst Arnauts and Greeks, from Albania's land,

With Croats, Poles, and Cossacks, have joined the

    band,

      And a score of tribes besides.

There were chiefs from the far-off Daghistan,

And Scythian bows from the Caspian ;

With warriors from Ethiopian lands,

And Bedouins dark from Arabia's sands,

　　　Who bend no cringing knee.

E'en the mail'd Circassian from El Burz * height

Has left his mountain to join in the fight,

With the sturdy Sikh, and the brave Affghan,

And men from the confines of Hindostan,

　　　To die in Islam's cause.

There were subtle Persians from Iran's shore,

With Kuzzilbash, Tartar, and many more,

Of every clime, and of every place,

Whatever their creed, whatever their race,

　　　Who spurned a tyrant's yoke.

* El Burz—the highest mountain of the Caucasus.

Though of different tongues, and of varied hue,

Each to each other prove kind and true ;

They own but one law, acknowledge no sway

But the will of a chief, whom all obey,

        At a sign from his flashing eyes.

A thousand bright swords are at his command,

A thousand steeds tether'd around him stand,

A thousand bold spirits obey his will,

To save and defend, or destroy and kill,

        As his mandate may decree.

By his black hair tent reclined the Bey,

Inhaling the fumes of a narguilhey ;*

And round their leader, with fragrant chibouks,

Lay the other chiefs of Bashi-Bazouks,

        Reposing at fall of day.

* Narguilhey—A water-pipe, or hookah.

His sunburnt brow a low green turban bore,
Wreath'd lightly round the crimson fez he wore;
O'er silken haik and gold-embroider'd vest
His jet-black beard fell flowing down his breast,
       A symbol of his rank.

Over his robe the white burnoose was hung,
Down from his side a heavy sabre swung;
A Cashmere shawl was twisted round his waist,
Where keen knife glitter'd amid pistols brac'd,
       On which his fingers played.

On the richest carpet of Iran's loom
Reclined a figure in earliest bloom,
Whose sylph-like form, and merry sparkling eyes,
Was the Bey's loved and far most valued prize,
       For she was passing fair.

No yashmac* now her lovely face conceals,
The close antena † her budding form reveals ;
And time can never from my mind erase
Her wondrous beauty and her form of grace,
   Which words cannot express.

So seeming gentle, and with mien so fair,
She brav'd dangers others would not dare ;
And more than once her fond devotion prov'd,
When hidden peril threaten'd him she lov'd,
   And dangers round them lurked.

How came that flower amid so wild a horde ?
(That none knew in the camp, save but her lord.)
Him she awaits, prepared is his repast,
With Ramzan's setting sun he'll break his fast,
   As the Prophet Chief decrees.

* Yashmac—The veil worn over the face by the Mussulmannee
women.
† Antena—A close-fitting boddice.

As she lay counting o'er her amber beads,

Dreaming of scenes of war and manly deeds,

The tent door open'd, and a Nubian slave

Unto her gentle mistress warning gave

Of her lord's footsteps nigh.

The blood now mantled to her blushing cheek,

Telling a tale that love alone could speak ;

She rose, look'd up, then sprang to his embrace,

And in his bosom hid her glowing face,

Beaming with mutual flame.

Her raven hair, in loose, dishevell'd charms,

Fell flowing, in thick tresses, o'er her arms,

Veiling her yielding form, as he caress'd,

And she sank lovingly upon his breast,

And kissed his swarthy brow.

Oh ! lengthened days of inglorious ease

Are well resigned for such joys as these ;

Pleasure flies quickly, too quickly away—

To-morrow mayn't come—be happy to-day,

  For who can read his fate ?

Some men find pleasure in riches and halls ;

And women, they tell me, " in toilette and balls."

Some say, " they are happy over their books,"

But I love the life of the Bashi-Bazouks,

  And the land of the sunny East.

H.M.S. " Spiteful," on voyage from Varna to the Crimea.

THE VOICE OF A FLOWER.

Lines written in a lady's album, below a lily of the valley which the author picked up the eve after the battle of Alma, close by Lieut.-Colonel Chester's grave.

> " Let us
> Find out the prettiest dasied spot we can,
> And make him, with our pikes and partizans,
> A grave."
>
> CYMBELINE.

————◆◇◆————

LADY! I come from distant lands,

    Belonging to the Czar,

And there I saw thy country's bands

    Victorious in the war.

For I beheld a fearful sight

    One bright September day,

When the Allies storm'd the height,

    And Russia's hosts gave way.

The Alma's banks with bright steel shone,
  And cannon frown'd on high;
Still the Allies came pressing on,
  To conquer or to die.

I saw the Zouaves, brave sons of France,
  Climbing the beetling height:
I saw their Eagles fast advance,
  Impatient for the fight.

I heard the Britons' shrill, wild cheer,
  I saw their bayonets gleam,
As "the red line," devoid of fear,
  Dash'd through the Alma's stream.

I heard the cannon open then
  'Gainst their devoted force:
The plain was strew'd with fallen men,
  Still they maintain'd their course,

'Mid clouds of smoke, through shot and grape,
   They forced the deadly way;
Though grim death lour'd in ev'ry shape,
   Nought could their progress stay.

I heard, amid the cannon's roar,
   Their heart-inspiring cry;
And up the height the Guardsmen tore,
   And charg'd the battery.

I saw the gallant Scotch Brigade,
   With music at their head,
March steadily, as on parade,
   Though scores of men fell dead.

Then loud uprose the Russian yell
   Above the battle's roar,
And hundreds round the earthwork fell,
   Welt'ring in their gore.

H

No danger stay'd those fearless men,
  Or check'd their bold career;
They closed their ranks and charged again—
  Those Isles-men knew no fear.

The Russians broke—they could not stand
  The Allies' fearful fire;
And in dismay their shatter'd band
  'Gan slowly to retire.

I saw the Czar's dense legions fly
  And the Allies advance;
Then loud uprose the Britons' cry,
  With shouts of "Vive la France!"

The sun had sunk low in the west,
  Ere the red fight was won;
Many a soldier lay at rest,
  Whose earthly course was run.

Many a warrior, grim and bold,
   Smiled in his latest breath;
Many a youth lay stiff and cold,
   Still lovely e'en in death.

Strange sounds were borne upon the breeze,
   From the dark rolling surge;
The wind was sighing 'mid the trees,
   Like melancholy dirge.

I grew upon the Alma's height,
   Above dark Euxine's waves,
And I was cull'd after the fight
   From 'midst the new-made graves.

And he who pluck'd me from the plain,
   Did so with deep-drawn sigh;
For 'mid the foremost of the slain,
   He'd seen a dear friend die.

Comrades stood round the soldier's grave,
    And breath'd a heartfelt prayer,
When one who mourn'd the fallen brave
    Pluck'd me as I grew there.

And thrust me to his throbbing heart,
    A souvenir of woe,
And of his friend's last earthly rest,
    Who perish'd 'mid the foe.

Lady! though dead, I once was fair,
    As aught of mortal birth :
Thou, too, fleeting charms may'st share—
    Listen ! O child of earth !

Like thee, once bloomed this faded flower,
    An emblem of mankind :
Hear, then, its voice, "The passing hour
    Is fleeting as the wind."

Thy beauty, too, will pass away,
　　And wither like a leaf,
, Or slowly fade to rank decay,
　　When death will bring relief.

The longest life is but a breath,
　　And like a valley's flower:
Thou too must pass the vale of death—
　　Prepare to meet that hour.

Scutari Hospital.

THE HIGHLANDER'S FAREWELL.

"Farewell! God knows when we shall meet again.
I have a faint cold fear thrills through my veins,
That almost freezes up the heat of life."

ROMEO AND JULIET.

———◆———

FARE-YE-WEEL, my Jeanie dear!

The hour is come to part.

Hark! the touns-folk, how they cheer!

Ye maunna' cry, sweetheart.

List, our Hieland music plays,

"The girls we left behind."

Oft that air, in future days,

Will bring auld friens to mind.

Fare-ye-weel, my Jeanie dear!

The hour is come to part.

Hark! the touns-folk, how they cheer!

Ye maunna' cry, sweetheart.

Dry your tears, my only love,
    And dinna, dinna weep:
Ken ye no' there's Ane above,
    Wha's gudeness ne'er will sleep?
Duty calls, I maun obey,
    And to my Queen pruve true.
Fare-ye-weel! I daurna stay—
    Sweetheart, ance mair, adieu.

    Fare-ye-weel, my Jeanie dear!
      The hour is come to part.
    Hark! the touns-folk, how they cheer!
      Ye maunna' cry, sweetheart.

Camp of Highland Brigade, Heights above Balaklava.

THE SONG OF THE FUSILIER.

"Cowards die many times before their deaths;
The valiant never taste of death but once.
Of all the wonders that I yet have heard,
It seems to me most strange that men should fear;
Seeing that death, a necessary end,
Will come when it will come."

JULIUS CÆSAR.

You have ask'd for my song, and your call I obey,

For perhaps it may serve to drive dull care away;

Join loud in the chorus, let the enemy hear,

That the eve before action our hearts knew no fear.

Fill the goblet again, fill it up to the brink,

For to some it may be the last cup they may drink;

Let our last night be gay, and drive away sorrow,

For why should a soldier think of to-morrow?

Now the sun is gone down, and no moon's gentle light
Sheds her silvery gleam through the dark murky night ;
Bright flashes of cannon blaze red 'gainst the sky,
And rockets are hissing through the air as they fly.

    Fill the goblet again, fill it up to the brink,
    For to some it may be the last cup they may drink ;
    Let our last night be gay, and drive away sorrow,
    For why should a soldier think of to-morrow ?

By the Alma's fam'd stream we have humbled the foe,
And at Balaklava their horsemen laid low ;
In Tchernaya's valley their battalions have fled,
And bleak Inkermann's height lay heaped with their dead.

    Fill the goblet again, fill it up to the brink,
    For to some it may be the last cup they may drink ;
    Let our last night be gay, and drive away sorrow,
    For why should a soldier think of to-morrow ?

We fought for Old England, for our Queen, and her crown,
No stain shall dishonour our ancient renown.
We may die!—who will not? yet what soldier will shrink
To pledge me " The morrow," the last toast he may drink?

> Fill the goblet again, fill it up to the brink,
> For to some it may be the last cup they may drink;
> Let our last night be gay, and drive away sorrow,
> For why should a soldier think of to-morrow?

Now the time's near at hand for bold deeds to be done,
The walls are now shaken, and the town must be won,
The morn is approaching, the assault now draws nigh;
I pledge ye " The morrow—may we conquer or die!"

> Fill the goblet again, fill it up to the brink,
> For to some it may be the last cup they may drink;
> Let our last night be gay, and drive away sorrow,
> For why should a soldier think of to-morrow?

Gordon's Battery before Sevastopol.

THE BRITON'S SONG.

"England, with all thy faults, I love thee still."

———◆———

THERE'S a magical charm in the land of our birth,
Which, seek where you will, is not found else on earth;
You may search till you tire, from the pole to the zone,
But where will you find any land like our own?
Her daughters are fairest, and what nation dare brave
The Isles-men of Britain, the queen of the wave;
I have roam'd through the world, but I cannot compare
Any men with her sons, any maids with her fair.

Then fill up your bumpers, and drink to my toast,
I pledge ye "The Island" we all love the most:
The gem of the ocean, the pride of the earth,
The bulwark of freedom, the land of our birth.

The red cross of Britain is the pride of the main,

An emblem of freedom, a flag without stain;

Go search through creation, on the land o'er the wave,

That standard ne'er floats o'er the head of a slave.

Like a meteor it shines, for 'tis borne to the field

By those who may die, but who never will yield;

Go search in Fame's volume, you'll find there its story,

And Britain's fair name, midst a halo of Glory.

Then fill up your bumpers, and drink to my toast,

I pledge ye " The Island " we all love the most:

The gem of the ocean, the pride of the earth,

The bulwark of freedom, the land of our birth.

Camp of the Naval Brigade, before Sevastopol.

HOMEWARD BOUND.

The following lines were written upon an incident of the late war, an account of which appeared in one of the English newspapers. A transport, conveying the wounded soldiers from the Crimea, had been telegraphed as having arrived at Spithead. No sooner was the anchor down than the vessel was crowded by the friends and relatives of the invalids, and among them came an old gentleman to look after the disembarkation of his only son, a youth of eighteen, who had been reported among the severely wounded. On arrival on board, the afflicted father was told that his son had breathed his last the evening before, within sight of land. The shock was too great for the old man to bear, and he died suddenly on hearing the news.

> "Soldier, rest! thy warfare o'er,
> Sleep the sleep that knows not breaking;
> Dream of battled fields no more,
> Days of danger, nights of waking."
>
> Scott.

THE sun was sinking in the west

  Below the deep-blue sea;

His rays still gilt the billows' crest,

  And land lay on our lee.

Darkly it loom'd above the wave,

  As twilight gather'd round;

Each heart was sad, each soldier grave,

  Though we were homeward bound.

For one all loved lay on the deck
    Who never would rise more;
His eyes were fix'd on that dark speck
    They said was England's shore.
His brow was chill—all pain was past—
    Tears stood in every eye;
The shades of death were gathering fast—
    His time was come to die.

His heart was in his father's hall,
    He fancied friends were nigh;
At times he'd on his mother call,
    And bid her not to sigh.
We heard him try to breathe the prayer
    Which she perchance had taught:
Veterans wept, as they stood there,
    With whom that boy had fought.

The night closed round—a mournful wail
  Was heard along the deep;
To all on board it told the tale—
  Our friend had sunk to sleep.
Bright morning broke—the fresh'ning breeze
  Our good ship onward bore;
We saw the cliffs and stately trees
  Of dear Old England's shore.

The anchor fell with grating sound;
  Our perils now were o'er,
And dear ones greet the homeward-bound
  They'd thought to see no more.
Friends crowded round : one hale old man
  Gazed on with troubled air;
Each soldier's face he seemed to scan,
  But no one knew him there.

At last he breathed the lost one's name—
    Each soldier turned away.
Again he ask'd—the captain came,
    But knew not what to say.
A tear rolled from the sailor's eye—
    He pointed o'er his head,
Where Britain's banner, half-mast high,
    Proclaimed that one was dead.

He took the mourner by the hand,
    And led him to the corse;
Surrounded by our weeping band,
    He told him of his loss.
The old man kissed the pallid cheek,
    And knelt down by the dead,
As if in prayer: he did not speak.
    He rose not—life had fled.

Scutari Hospital.

THE BASHI-BAZOUK TO HIS HORSE,
"DESERT-BORN."

"He paweth in the valley, and rejoiceth in his strength; he goeth on to meet the armed men.

"He mocketh at fear, and is not affrighted; neither turneth he back from the sword."—JOB.

COME, rouse thee, my charger, prepare for the fray,

For trumpets are braying, and we must away!

The booming of cannon sounds loud on the wind;

When fame's to be won, we must ne'er be behind.

Let those who prefer it dwell in a fix'd home,

But we, my heart's treasure, together will roam!

For Islam is threaten'd—the Sultan has need

Of the Bashi-bazouk and his brave Arab steed.

I'm mounted! I'm mounted! I'm away like the wind;

No steed in the desert can leave me behind.

Al-ham-du-lillah!*—I fear not a foe;

I'm free as the breezes that o'er the sands blow!

* "Thanks be to God!" a common Arabic expression.

I

My own " Desert-born," dost remember the day,

When Cossack hordes hovered around us at bay,

And we charg'd through the mass like a whirlwind's blast,

And gained the vast steppe when the danger was past?

How the foes howled with rage as they watched our flight,

And followed our course till the fall of the night?

I laughed at their efforts—for, unmatched in speed,

I knew none could reach us, my brave Arab steed!

    I'm mounted! I'm mounted! I'm away like the wind;

    No steed in the desert can leave me behind.

    Al-ham-du-lillah!—I fear not a foe;

    I'm free as the breezes that o'er the sands blow!

We've traversed the land, and we've sailed o'er the main—

Now the hour's near at hand to set forth again.

Fearless of danger, we roam in all weather;

No peril can daunt us while we are together

No maiden so fair but she causes remorse:

I have known none with thee, my own gallant horse!

I never found friend in the hour of my need

True as thee, "Desert-born," my brave Arab steed!

I'm mounted! I'm mounted! I'm away like the wind;

No steed in the desert can leave me behind.

Al-ham-du-lillah!—I fear not a foe;

I'm free as the breezes that o'er the sands blow!

Camp Alah-deen, near Varna.

THE WOUNDED HIGHLANDER.

" I am a soldier, and unapt to weep,
　Or to exclaim on fortune's fickleness."

HENRY VI.

————◦◦◦————

RECITATIVE.

THE eve the Alma's heights were won,
　As o'er the field I trod,
I marked a wounded Highlander
　Lie bleeding on the sod.
His brother strove to stanch the wound;
　Alas! it was in vain:
Dark crimson streams flow'd on the ground;
　And he sang this sad strain :—

"Ye maunna weep for me, Willie!
　O dinna greet sae sair:
Ye'll follow me ere lang, laddie,
　When we shall part nae mair!
Like yonder setting sun, Willie,
　E'en sae my course is run;
But he will rise again, laddie,
　And I shall then be gone!

"Maybe when ye'll gae back, Willie,
　To our hame by the burn,
Ye'll tell them a' the tale, laddie,
　O' him wha'll no return.
Ye'll tell them how I foucht, Willie,
　Like sodger, true and brave!
'Twill ease my mither's heart, laddie,
　When I am in the grave.

" There's ane wha sair will greet, Willie—

The news, oh ! gently break,

For she was a' in a' to me ;

Ye'll lo'e her for my sake !

Oh but it's hard to dee, Willie,

And leave her a' alane !

It's but for her I greet, laddie—

For her when I am gane.

" Oh dinna mind my words, Willie,

And dinna, dinna sigh ;

I wadna ca' life back again—

'Tis for my Queen I die !

And 'tis a glorious day, Willie,

As e'er yon sun set on.

Ye'll comfort a' at hame, laddie,

When I am deid an' gone !

" Now fauld me to your heart, Willie,

    The nicht air's fearfu' keen !

And kiss me ere I gae, laddie !

    There's darkness o'er my een.

I ken I'm sinking fast, Willie,

    The cauld strikes to the bane !

Ye'll comfort a' at hame, laddie,

    When I am deid an' gane !"

Close in his brother's arms,

    Locked in his fast embrace,

He passed away as if in sleep,

    A smile upon his face.

We cut a lock of curling hair

    That o'er his brow did wave ;

Then by the Alma's rippling stream

    We dug the soldier's grave.

Camp, Valley of Balbec.

THE OLD SONG.

"That old and antique song we heard last night;
Methought it did relieve my passion much :
More than light airs and recollected terms,
Of these most brisk and giddy-paced times."

TWELFTH NIGHT.

THERE's something in the well-known tone

Of ancient ballad lays,

That calls to mind, though years have flown,

The friends of early days.

I've seen them cause the tears to start

From sternest soldier's eye ;

No modern strains could touch his heart

Like those of days gone by.

Then sing to me the songs of yore,

For though they make me sigh,

They bring to mind dear friends once more,

And happy days gone by.

I love to hear the ancient lays
  My mother used to sing;
They tell me of my childhood's days,
  And fond thoughts backwards bring.

I dream of days of hope and joy
  Whene'er I hear that strain;
I think that I am still a boy,
  And hear her voice again.

    Then sing to me the songs of yore,
      For though they make me sigh,
    They bring to mind dear friends once more,
      And happy days gone by.

Camp of the Guards, Balaklava.

THE WOUNDED TROOPER TO HIS SWORD.

" Behold, I have a weapon ;
A better never did itself sustain
Upon a soldier's thigh : I have seen the day,
That, with this little arm and this good sword,
I have made my way through more impediments
Than twenty times your stop :—But, O vain boast !
Who can control his fate? 'tis not so now."

OTHELLO.

Adieu, old friend, my work is o'er,

I'm fading like a leaf ;

I ne'er may dare the combat more,

So slumber in thy sheath.

No more I'll hear the trumpet bray,

Or rollings of the drum ;

I hear my charger fondly neigh ;

Alas! I cannot come.

Hast thou forgot, my well-tried brand,

    That morn, when full of pride,

I took thee from my father's hand,

    And girt thee to my side—

How the old man his blessing poured,

    As I bade him adieu ?

Since then thou'st flashed when battles roared,

    No friend e'er proved more true.

On India's plain thou'st often shone

    In many a sturdy fight;

When the fierce Khalsa's lands were won,

    And Britain showed her might.

Thou glisten'd by the Alma's rill,

    In Balaklava's vale ;

Of Inkermann's bleak blood-stain'd hill,

    Thou too couldst tell the tale.

I hear a voice in every breeze
   That steals along the sea,
Amid the murmurings of the trees,
   There's something speaks to me.
It seems to say, "Thy last field's fought,
   The summoner is nigh;"
The brightest days are ever short,
   I have no cause to sigh.

My eyes grow dim—the time's at hand
   When e'en thine aid is vain;
Yet thanks to thee, my trusty brand,
   My honour knows no stain.
Why should I reck my hour is come,
   Old friends have gone before,
My duty done—fair fame is won,
   What would a soldier more?

Scutari Hospital.

THE THREE TOASTS:

AN OUTPOST SONG.

"I looked upon her with a soldier's eye,
  That lik'd, but had a rougher task in hand
  Than to drive liking to the name of love."

  MUCH ADO ABOUT NOTHING.

SEND the grog-can round to-night,

  The wind blows bitter cold;

Stir the watch-fire, let the light

  Shine bright across the wold.

Let us sing a jovial song

  To pass the time away;

Soldiers' lives may not be long,

  Why should they not be gay?

    Let us sing a jovial song

      To pass the time away;

    Soldiers' lives may not be long,

      Why should they not be gay?

Soldiers, wheresoe'er ye roam,

A name thrills in your breast;

Each has some one left at home

He loves above the rest.

Who among us does not think,

At times, of one most dear?

Fill your cans, and let us drink

"Her health," friends, with a cheer.

Let us sing a jovial song

To pass the time away;

Soldiers' lives may not be long,

Why should they not be gay?

Are there none at home to-night,

Who breathe a heart-felt prayer,

To Him who rules the sternest fight,

To keep us in his care?

Here's, then, to those we left at home,
   Our sweethearts and our wives—
Fathers, mothers, ev'ry one
   For whom we risk our lives.
      Let us sing a jovial song
         To pass the time away;
      Soldiers' lives may not be long,
         Why should they not be gay?

Still another verse I'll sing,
   Comrades, you'll own I'm right;
Who knows what the morrow 'll bring,
   So fill your cups this night.
Drink the health of her most dear,
   With me your voices blend,
In a shout the foe shall hear,
   " The Queen," the soldier's friend.
      Let us sing a jovial song
         To pass the time away;
      Soldiers' lives may not be long,
         Why should they not be gay?

Balaklava Col.

BALAKLAVA.

"The paths of glory lead but to the grave."

———◆———

LOUDLY the trumpets bray'd,

Each drew his battle-blade,

And England's Light Brigade

        Moved on to die.

"Forward!" cried Cardigan.

Onward rode ev'ry man;

Shot and shell then began

        On them to play.

" Forward !" their leaders cried,

" Huzza !" the men replied,

As they rode side by side

        Onwards to death.

No soldier fear'd to die,

No trooper made reply,

No craven turn'd to fly—

        Onwards all rode.

Onwards ! the Squadrons dash'd ;

Onwards ! though cannon flash'd ;

Onwards ! like whirlwinds crash'd

        Old England's horse.

Onwards ! in England's name ;

Onwards ! through smoke and flame ;

Onwards ! to deathless fame,

        Led Cardigan.

K

On! though death lay in wait;

On! spite of odds and fate;

On! still at desperate rate,

    Tore the Brigade.

On! with a British cheer;

On! without sign of fear;

On! in their bold career,

    Our troopers rode.

On! for our Old Renown;

On! for our Queen and Crown!

On! e'en though scores go down

    Stricken to earth.

On! as the tiger leaps,

On! as the typhoon sweeps,

On! o'er the dead in heaps,

    Our squadrons flew.

On! tore the Light Brigade,

Fearless, and undismay'd

O'er heads their sabres play'd

   As they advanced.

Though Death's jaws open'd wide,

Boot to boot, side by side,

Reckless, though many died,

   Onwards they tore.

They fear'd no Russian yell,

Heeded not shot or shell,

On through "a fire of hell,"

   Those brave hearts rode.

Brightly their sabres flash'd,

As mid the foe they dash'd,

Cheering as on they crash'd,

   Cutting their way.

Through Cossack hordes they tore,

Through Russian ranks they bore,

Through guns that loudly roar,

   Belching forth death.

No foe could stand their force,

No foe could stay their course,

No foe could face those horse

   In their career.

Though many leaders bled,

Though men and horse fell dead,

Though their best blood was shed,

   Still they fought on.

Chargers were breath'd and lam'd,

Troopers were tired and maim'd,

Nothing more could be gain'd,

   So they return'd.

Back came the Light Brigade,

Cannon upon them play'd,

Still firm and undismay'd

        The remnant rode.

Riderless o'er the plain,

Chargers with tossing mane,

Crimson with gory stain,

        Gallop'd about.

Troopers, whose steeds were slain,

Rush'd wildly o'er the plain,

Striving to catch the rein,

        As they tore by.

As lions force their way

Through hunters when at bay,

So our men broke that day

        Back through the foe.

Volleys were on them pour'd,

Cannon against them roar'd,

As they rode through the horde,

          Hewing a path.

Clouds of horse lined the way,

Cossacks yell'd round their prey,

But, stricken with dismay,

          They dar'd not stand.

When ours are " times of old,"

And we sleep in the mould,

Still will the tale be told

          Of that day's charge.

Nobly our troopers fought,

Dearly was Honour bought;

A lesson that day was taught

          To Britain's foes.

Cheeks will blanch, lips will pale,

When our friends hear the tale ;

For Balaklava's vale

   Was heap'd with dead.

Thirty score British horse

Started upon that course,

Of that devoted force

   A third return'd.

Light Cavalry Camp, Karani.

THE HUNGARIAN PATRIOT'S DEATH-SONG.

The following lines were written from an account given me by the late General Guyon (Korschid Pacha), as we sat one evening round a watch-fire on Kislar Dagh, a low hill overlooking Kars. A young Hungarian officer, who had been wounded in a skirmish, was taken prisoner by the Austrians, tried by a drum-head court-martial, condemned, and executed at an hour's notice. He died like a hero, without a single murmur at his untimely fate escaping from his lips.

"Come vedi—ancor non m'abbandona."—DANTE.

My fate is seal'd, the sentence past,

    The hour is come for me to die.

Still, oh, my soul! be not o'ercast;

    The tyrants must not hear a sigh.

Comrades, adieu!   Mourn not, my friend,

    A soldier ne'er should be cast down;

The darkest day must have an end,

    E'en Fortune cannot always frown.

Though I may die a felon's doom,

    Dishonour ne'er shall taint my name;

Laurels will gild the patriot's tomb,

    'Tis crime that makes a death of shame.

Forsake not, Lord, my Fatherland !

    E'en though we fall on stormy days,

" Who shall presume to understand

    The mighty wisdom of Thy ways?"

Oh, my country! Heaven aid thee,

    My latest thoughts, my dying prayer.

Death, though near, has not dismayed me,

    Hope still is left—I'll not despair.

I bless thee with my dying breath,

    For thee alone my heart now bleeds:

I'm ready now—I fear not death ;

    It has no pang when Honour leads.

General Guyon's Head-quarters, Kars.

AN ALARM IN CAMP.

One murky night in October, 1854, a rushing sound was heard like the galloping of cavalry in the valley of Balaklava, and the whole British camp got under arms, as also did our Allies. We remained in suspense for some few moments, not knowing which was the point of the enemy's attack, when suddenly two squadrons of *riderless* Russian horse charged along the road, and burst into our lines, in spite of a volley from the outposts, which killed several. They were soon caught, and proved to be the horses of two squadrons of Liprandi's cavalry, who had been panic-struck with *stampedo*, and rushed wildly towards our camp, where they had been previously quartered.

> " Tis the soldier's life
> To have their balmy slumbers wak'd with strife !"
>
> OTHELLO.

'TWAS eve.   Within a comrade's tent

Arose loud bursts of merriment.

The wine-cups chink'd as round they went,

      And toasts were drunk.

Old England's lays were sung that night:
Strange stories told of recent fight;
All there were gay, each heart was light,
        And mirth reign'd round.

The night came on.   A silence deep
Over the camp then seem'd to creep,
And round the fires all lay asleep,
        Without a care.

Time pass'd.   The day began to dawn;
When sullen sound of distant horn,
Upon the wind at times was borne.
        What can it mean?

The mists dispersed.   With morning's grey
A strange wild cry, a charger's neigh;
And distant sounds, like trumpets' bray,
        Came down the vale.

I noticed then my Arab steed,
A gallant grey of Nedjed's breed,
Turn away from his morning feed
       And snuff the air.

He understood the dubious sound,
And arch'd his neck and gaz'd around,
Then shook his mane, and paw'd the ground
       Impatiently.

Fire flash'd from out his sparkling eye,
He answer'd the defiant cry,
And shriek'd with joy as I drew nigh
       To loose his bonds.

Again the horn, a tramp, a hum;
Our videttes cry, "Turn out! they come!"
Then rang the bugle and the drum
       Through the valley.

At the first blast of that warning sound
Each soldier rose from off the ground,
Rubb'd his eyes and look'd around
            Wonderingly.

Throughout the camp "the alarm" rang,
On ev'ry side shrill trumpets sang,
Each trooper to his saddle sprang,
            Ready, aye ready.

The squadrons form'd without a word,
Each trooper drew his battle-sword,
And long'd to charge the Russian horde;
            But none were seen.

Sir Colin, with the Scotch brigade,
Drew up in line, and thus array'd,
Fear'd no foe's onset—undismayed,
            He watched events.

We mann'd our lines, nor watch'd in vain,

A cloud of dust swept o'er the plain,

And chargers tore with loosen'd rein,

     All *riderless.*

Amid our lines a way they sought,

Two hundred steeds were quickly caught;

They did not like the side they fought,

     And came to us.

                 Ottoman Camp, Balaklava Col.

THE KHABYLE EXILE.

During a skirmish on the Danube, near Turtakoi, in which the Bashi-bazouks successfully repulsed a superior number of Cossacks, one of them, who had been most conspicuous for his daring reckless bravery during the contest, was carried off the field on a litter, having received several sabre cuts. As he was borne along, I heard him lamenting that his wounds were not mortal; regretting that he had not been left to die, as he had nothing to live for. Having been particularly struck with his gallant conduct in the affair, I had him taken care of, and when he was recovered from his wounds, attached him to my person. One day he told me his story, which is the subject of the following lines. He was a Khabyle by birth, and had suffered from the unwarrantable barbarities committed by the French. He had seen his village sacked and burnt, and his family and friends murdered before his eyes; himself being severely wounded, and left on the field for dead. Having recovered from his wounds, he vowed eternal vengeance against the French, and joining the Emir Ab-d'hul-Kadir, was one of the most active in the war of retaliation in 1845, being present when Colonel Montagnac and 450 men were cut up (with the exception of fourteen who were taken prisoners) at the Marabout of Sidi Brahim. On the submission of the Emir, he fled from Algiers, and finding his way to Turkey, joined the Bashi-bazouks. He became very much attached to me, proving a devoted follower, "ever faithful to his salt." He did not, however, meet the death he desired in the field, but perished miserably of putrid fever in the Crimea, when starvation and pestilence reduced a force of nearly 7,000 men to little more than 1,800.

It is upon the battle-plain
  That I would wish to die ;
In stubborn contest I would yield
  My life without a sigh.
I would not die from length of years,
  And linger on in pain,
I'd rather fall where soldiers' tears
  Bedew a comrade slain.

I ne'er shall see my native land,
  I can no more return ;
My home is now a heap of sand ;
  I saw the hamlet burn.
I saw two brothers breathless lie,
  E'en though I strove to save ;
I saw my aged mother die
  Upon my father's grave.

I saw my comrades slaughter'd fall,
　I heard the women cry;
My blood that night was turn'd to gall—
　I've seen the grim foe die.
Go! listen to the Santon's tale,
　Ask how my vengeance fell,
When in Sidi Brahim's vale
　Was heard the Giaours' yell.

Revenge some time gave me relief;
　There's blood upon that brand;
But now my heart is bowed in grief
　To see my native land.
For traitor hearts have taken gold,
　And own the Giaour as lord;
Ishmael's birthright they have sold,
　And with it's gone the sword.

A curse upon the traitor knaves
　　Who wrought this deed of shame;
Defiled be their fathers' graves,
　　Detested be their name.
" May their tribe's mares be slow of speed,
　　Their daughters swift to fly;
A curse upon the dastard breed,
　　That knew not how to die!"

There is a wound which never heals,
　　That time can never cure,
It is the woe that "El Garb"* feels
　　The Frank yoke to endure.
I am an exile all alone,
　　And seek for rest in vain,
No friend will reck when I am gone,
　　Why linger on in pain?

---

* " El Garb," the West. The Arab name for Algiers, Morocco, and
Barbary.

Bright youthful hopes have vanish'd all ;

   And, like a faded leaf,

The time draws near when I should fall,

   The grave may bring relief.

Let Azrael* come, I care not when,

   I laugh at Fate's decree,

I've brav'd it over and again ;

   Death always flies from me.

Now ask me why thus, face to face,

   I seek to meet my fate ?

I am the last of all my race,

   And death e'en comes too late.

It is not that I crave the wreath

   A soldier strives to gain—

It is that I would rest in death,

   And leave this scene of pain.

* Azrael, the Angel of Death.

THE STANDARD.

The flag that's braved a thousand years
The battle and the breeze."

CAMPBELL.

The standard of Old England,

The emblem of the free,

Is waving on the castle keep

For a great victory.

The nation holds a festival

To welcome back the band,

Who 'gainst the foe have well maintained

The honour of the land.

Then cheer for merrie England,

The country of the free ;

And may her might defend the right

To all posterity.

The standard of Old England
   Is waving half-mast high,
And crowds have gathered in the streets
   To see the pageantry.
Beneath that flag our comrades fought
   And died, but not in vain ;
What tho' its folds are soiled and torn,
   Its honour knows no stain.

    Then cheer for merrie England,
      The country of the free ;
    And may her might defend the right
      To all posterity.

The standard of Old England,
   In every clime unfurled,
Has floated now a thousand years,
   And still defies the world.

In every sea that banner floats,
An honour to the wave;
Where'er it flutters in the breeze
Its shadow frees the slave.

Then cheer for merrie England,
The country of the free;
And may her might defend the right
To all posterity.

Camp of the Rifle Brigade, before Sevastopol.

THE BURIAL OF CATHCART.

KILLED ON THE FIFTH OF NOVEMBER, 1854, AT THE
BATTLE OF INKERMANN.

> O'er better knight, on death-bier laid,
> Torch never gleamed, nor mass was said.

— ◆ —

In England's camp soft music peals
   A requiem sad and slow;
Soldiers, gathering mournfully,
   In long procession go.
And minute-guns are booming,
   Standards wave half-mast high,
Their silken folds droop heavily
   Against the azure sky.

With arms reversed, and muffled drums,
    And martial music's strain,
A mourning band, with measur'd tread,
    Escort the noble slain.
Stern warriors' grief at last bursts forth,
    And bitter tears are shed;
Each soldier feels his heart is full,
    He knows *a friend* is dead.

Upon the carriage of a gun
    Is borne the warrior's corse,
And with a proud and stately gait
    Is led his battle-horse.
On the bier lie cap and sabre,
    A standard is the pall;
And slowly moves the cortége on
    To the Dead March in Saul.

Now the priests have said the prayer
    For a departed soul;
Volleys flash red through the air,
    And muffled drums loud roll;
Still mourners linger on the hill,
    And speak in under-tone;
For who shall fill the place of him,
    The Chieftain who is gone?

His hour came—he pass'd away,
    The dauntless and the brave;
In victory's proud moment
    He found a soldier's grave.
Many a red field had he seen,
    Many a battle won;
But now his last fight's over,
    The hero's course is run.

He died as a soldier should,

    In harness, sword in hand,

Surrounded by the enemy,

    And cheering on his band.

What a glorious fate was his!

    Why reck?   His work was done—

He'd past the autumn of his life;

    He fell—as sets the sun.

In after years when we shall meet,

    Survivors of the fray,

Memory will bring back to us

    The friends we lost that day;

And when the wine-cup passes round,

    As long as two remain,

Again we'll fight the battle o'er,

    And think upon the slain.

Then to our sons we'll tell the tale,

   How Inkermann was won ;

And of the gallant feats that day

   By British soldiers done.

We'll think upon that low bleak hill,

   Where many comrades lie,

The burial-place of Britain's dead,

   The pride of chivalry.

Scutari Hospital.

SECOND SIGHT :

A TALE OF THE WAR.

These lines were written on an incident which appeared in one of the Scotch papers. A young girl, who was sinking from rapid decline, on the eve of Inkermann had a presentiment that her lover was slain, and she died, assuring her mother that she heard his voice calling to her on the gale. When the news of the victory arrived, his name was found in the Gazette amongst the slain.

> " Can this be death ? there's bloom upon her cheek ;
> But now I see it is no living hue,
> But a strange hectic—like the unnatural red
> Which autumn plants upon the perish'd leaf."
>
> MANFRED.

CHILD.

The night is closing round, mother ;

The wind howls sadly deep ;

I dread that moaning sound, mother—

I cannot, dare not, sleep.

MOTHER.

Night winds are whisp'ring deep, my child,
   And round us strangely wail;
But calm thy mind to sleep, my child,
   They cannot thee assail.

CHILD.

Strange dreams are coming on, mother;
   Hark! listen to the breeze!
Oh! heard ye not a voice, mother,
   Sighing amid the trees?

MOTHER.

'Tis but November's gale, my child;
   You have no cause to fear.
Why heed the tempest's wail, my child?—
   It cannot reach you here.

CHILD.

'Tis his voice in the breeze, mother;
  I heard it as I lay.
Oh! help me to my knees, mother—
  I feel I ought to pray.

MOTHER.

Pray in thy mother's arms, my child—
  Repose upon this breast;
I'll sing to you "his song," my child—
  'Twill lull you into rest.

CHILD.

He's fallen in the fight, mother,
  Mid comrades true and brave;
Upon a cold, bleak height, mother,
  Is dug my Willie's grave.

MOTHER.

'Tis but a fearful dream, my child—

    A fantasy of mind;

God watches over him, my child—

    Fear not the howling wind.

CHILD.

No! he himself was here, mother;

    He kiss'd me as I lay;

I feel I'm going too, mother—

    You would not wish me stay.

MOTHER.

Oh! cease this fearful tale, my child—

    It smites me to the brain;

Heed not a wild wind's wail, my child—

    Let it not cause thee pain.

CHILD.

Death has no pangs to me, mother—
    It comes like gentle sleep;
Your face I cannot see, mother—
    All round is darkness deep.

I feel that thou art near, mother—
    I hear thee sob and cry;
I have not any fear, mother—
    I know my Willie's nigh.

Oh! do not, do not weep, mother—
    Cease those heartrending sighs;
'Tis but a gentle sleep, mother,
    That's stealing o'er my eyes.

Kiss me, kiss me again, mother,

    Once more before I die ;

I have not any pain, mother—

    Good-bye, mother! good-bye !

MOTHER.

Oh ! art thou really gone, my child ?—

    I do not feel thy breath ;

I cannot live alone, my child—

    Take me too—O grim Death !

Thou'rt gone to join thy love, my child,

    And I must not repine ;

We yet shall meet above, my child—

    " God's will be done—not mine."

Scutari Hospital.

LOVE-SONG.

A TRANSLATION FROM THE ARABIC.

" Do not swear at all ;
  Or if thou wilt, swear by thy gracious self,
  Which is the god of my idolatry,
  And I'll believe thee."

ROMEO AND JULIET.

————◦◦◦————

Dost thou ask me if I love thee?
  Maiden with the flowing hair ;
By Great Allah now above me,
  Thee alone I love, I swear.

If I e'er do aught to grieve thee,
  Maiden with the laughing eyes,
May my right hand's cunning leave me,
  Valueless be all I prize.

May my Nedjed charger fail me,

    Maid with locks of sable hue;

May my comrades coward hail me,

    If I ever prove less true.

May hieries* die and lose their speed,

    Maiden, fairest of the west;

May friends forsake in time of need,

    If I love not thee the best.

May my banner down be riven,

    Like a craven let me die,

Curs'd alike by man and Heaven,

    If I give thee cause to sigh.

Camp of the Second Division,
    Heights of Inkermann.

---

* Camels of high caste, celebrated for their speed and great endurance.

THE HIGHLANDER'S BETROTHED.

"But she so loves the token,
(For he conjur'd her she would ever keep it,)
That she reserves it ever more about her
To kiss and talk to."

OTHELLO.

My heart is sair, I canna rest,

   I'm no mysel' at a' at a';

The sodger lad I lo'e the best

   Is o'er the seas far far awa'.

Thinking a' nicht o' him I love,

   I canna close my aching e'e;

But pray to Him wha rules above

   To guard the absent o'er the sea.

They tell me that I ance was fair,

    But noo my cheeks are growing wan ;

I dinna heed—why should I care ?

    For joy has fled noo Willie's gane.

My mither bids me no' to weep,

    And fayther aye speaks kind to me ;

Still frae my hame I aften creep,

    And greet for ane far o'er the sea.

A gowden coin in twa we brak

    The eve afore he left the burn ;

He kissed my broo, nae word he spak—

    God grant that he may safe return !

I canna sleep, my heart is sair,

    And gin he come no' I shall dee ;

Baith morn an' eve I breathe a prayer

    For my brave Willie o'er the sea.

Camp of Highland Brigade,
Heights above Balaklava.

THE DYING GIRL TO HER BETROTHED.

"The angels, not half so happy in heaven,
  Went envying her and me;
Yes! that was the reason (as all men know,
  In this kingdom by the sea)
That the wind came out of the cloud by night,
  Chilling and killing my Annabel Lee."

EDGAR ALLAN POE.

Let me sit on your knee, laddie.

  My heart is fu' o' care,

And gaze upon your face, laddie,

  I soon shall see nae mair.

Oh! lay your cheek to mine, laddie,

  And tell me I'm your ain;

Ye'll think betimes o' me, laddie,

  When I am deid and gane.

I wadna hae ye greet, laddie,

   Nor let your grief be sair ;

Ye ken ere lang we'll meet, laddie,

   To part again nae mair.

Noo, clasp me in your arms, laddie,

   Ance mair ere we twa part ;

Ye'll think betimes o' me, laddie,

   Your ain puir fond sweetheart.

R. A. M. S. Macgregor Laird,
Off Madeira.

SHADOWS.

" There was but one beloved face on earth,
  And that was shining on him; he had look'd
Upon it till it could not pass away
He had no breath, no being, but in hers:
She was his voice; he did not speak to her,
But trembled on her words: she was his sight,
For his eye followed hers, and saw with hers,
Which colour'd all his objects:—he had ceased
To live within himself; she was his life."

As racked with pain I sleepless lie,

My soul recalls the past,

And conjures up with magic power

Those days too bright to last.

In vain time spreads its misty veil

O'er scenes of bygone years;

Memory drives away the clouds,

And all that was appears.

Oft at weird midnight's silent hour
   Shadowy hosts I see,
And one who dwells in Spirit Land
   Comes here to comfort me.
Like a star that has drifted earthward,
   She leaves the spheres on high,
To guide my soul to that blessed land
   Where love can never die.

The hum and din of earthly sounds
   Ring loudly on thine ear;
Thou canst not hear the whisperings
   That summon me from here.
A dreamless sleep is stealing on,
   I feel the end is nigh;
The chain has snapped—my soul is free—
   The hour has come—Good-bye!

Scutari Hospital.

YOUTHFUL DAYS.

" We were, fair queen,
Two lads that thought there was no more behind,
But such a day to-morrow as to-day,
And to be boy eternal."

WINTER'S TALE.

Autumn leaves are falling fast,

And winter now draws nigh—

Brightest days are soonest past,

So seize them as they fly.

Youth is like a limpid stream

Fast flowing to the main ;

Passing like a fleeting dream

That never comes again.

Youth is like the bright sunshine

   Upon a summer's day;

Childhood is a happy time

   That flies too soon away.

Years roll on and bring alloy,

   And life is overcast,

Then we find our hopes of joy

   With youthful days are past.

Cavalry Camp, Eupatoria.

TO MY CHARGER, "DESERT-BORN."

KILLED AT THE BATTLE OF INKERMANN, 5TH NOVEMBER, 1854.

" Day glimmers on the dying and the dead,
The cloven cuirass, and the helmless head ;
The war-horse masterless is on the earth,
And that last gasp hath burst his bloody girth ;
And near, yet quivering with what life remain'd,
The heel that urged him and the hand that rein'd."

LARA.

"DESERT-BORN " was an Arab steed,

A noble grey, of sacred breed ;

Rear'd on the plains of Nedjed's lands,

Of race far-famed through El-Garb's sands ;

Enduring in the longest chase,

His speed ne'er knew a second place ;

He was all that a steed should be,

And I lov'd him and he lov'd me.

With pedigree unsoil'd by stains,

The purest blood ran through his veins ;

And he could boast of lineage higher

Than royalty can e'er aspire.

The dam whence sprang his royal line

Mahomed bore, that chief divine,

Who in Medina taught to pray,

And in bless'd Mecca pass'd away.

In danger's hour, in longest ride,

No rowels touch'd my charger's side.

He knew my voice—a single word

Could urge him on, swift as a bird.

Oft when, at eve, our toil was done,

And we repos'd at set of sun,

My steed would whine to be caress'd,

Then by my side lay down to rest.

At Inkermann my charger fell,

Stricken to earth by bursting shell.

No truer comrade fell that day

Than "Desert-born," my gallant grey.

He lov'd his master, ne'er deceived—

O'er dearer friend man never griev'd;

For, in the hour of utmost need,

None prov'd so true as my poor steed.

Scutari Hospital.

THE VETERAN'S SONG.

"The few whom war and time have spared
  Are feeble, old, and grey;
And for myself, why let it pass,
  For I have had my day."

THE STORMING OF SAN SEBASTIAN.

WE were boys thegether,

  Like birdies in a nest;

Ance mair in native heather,

  We'll lay us doun to rest.

The gude auld man, the cheersome dame,

  In the cauld kirkyard lie,

An' youthfu' friens are a' gane hame—

  Still, frien, we maunna sigh.

We grew up bairns thegether,

Like birdies on the wing;

Your heart was like a feather,

And still, auld frien, we sing.

We baith hae pass'd our manhood's prime,

And gane throngh cares and joys;

Yet a's noo chang'd since that gay time

When you and I were boys.

We twa hae foucht thegether,

In battle side by side;

We've brav'd baith wind and weather,

When comrades round have died.

Though noo we poor and frienless stand,

Nae care our peace destroys;

We've foucht and conquer'd for the land

We lov'd when we were boys.

Camp, Kamara.

THE PLAGUE-STRICKEN SOLDIER'S SONG.

"Every wight has his weird, and we maun a' dee when our day comes."—Rob Roy.

————✦————

O DEATH! and dost thou come at last
    In strange and ghastly form?
Oft by my head thy dart hast past
    Amid the battle's storm.

I've seen it strike my comrades brave,
    As they fought by my side;
I envy them their soldier's grave—
    Ah! would I so had died!

N

I never fear'd thy glancing shaft,
    E'en though it graz'd my brow;
In direst peril I have laugh'd—
    Think not to scare me now.

Though I had hoped upon the field
    To meet a soldier's death,
'Twas not my fate, and I must yield,
    In sickness. my last breath.

Strange darkness now obscures my sight,
    A chill creeps o'er my frame;
Adieu to all my visions bright!
    Farewell, all hopes of fame!

Scutari Hospital.

DEATH-SONG OF A CIRCASSIAN CHIEF.

Written whilst in camp at Tshamshira to a wild air chanted by the retainers of Prince Michael, the Suzerain of Abassia.

> "O, farewell!
> Farewell the neighing steed, and the shrill trump,
> The spirit-stirring drum, the ear-piercing fife,
> The royal banner; and all quality,
> Pride, pomp, and circumstance of glorious war!"
>
> OTHELLO.

Farewell! my comrades true;

My work is done:

My race is won—

Adieu, my friends, adieu!

Farewell! my gallant horse.

No more we'll dash

Where sabre's flash—

No more we'll run a course.

Farewell! my faithful hound.

You'll whine in vain,

To hear again

Your master's footsteps sound.

Farewell! my trusty sword.

No more thy steel

Will cause to reel

The faithless Giaour's horde.

Farewell! my trumpet's blast.

My hour is come ;

The goal is won ;

My bright career is past.

Farewell ! my only son.

 For thy sire's sake

 Thou'lt vengeance take :

Remember it be done.

Farewell, Amina's love !

 You'll think of me,

 Where'er you be,

And join me—there—above.

Farewell, my tribe, farewell !

 No more my steed

 Thy ranks shall lead—

Revenge my death.   Farewell !

Omar Pacha's Camp,
Tshamshira.

THE ALMA.

A DIRGE.

" Why, then, God's soldier be he !
Had I as many sons as I have hairs,
I would not wish them to a fairer death :
And so his knell is knoll'd."

MACBETH.

THERE is a spot far o'er the waves,

O'er Euxine's dark and murky shore,

Where, sleeping in their unknown graves,

Lie friends whom we shall meet no more.

The place is hallow'd where they lie,

Fame will ever tell their story;

In England's cause they dared to die

By the Alma—Europe's glory.

Mourn for the brave who that day fell ;

    Lament, Old Albion's daughters ;

For many sleep, who loved you well

    By the Alma's bloody waters.

A vacant seat by some fire-side

    Oft recalls a soldier's story,

Who for his Queen and country died

    By the Alma—Europe's glory.

Spread the tidings far and wide,

    How gallantly our Allies fought,

When they scaled that steep hill-side,

    And with their life-blood honour bought.

Say how Zouave and Arab dying,

    On that field so red and gory,

With our own brave sons are lying

    By the Alma—Europe's glory.

Camp, Kamara.

THE AULD RUSKIE CZAR.

An impromptu song, written to the air of " The Laird o' Cockpen,"
which song had just been sung by a Scotch engineer, who was in the
only vessel that escaped at Sinope.

THE auld Ruskie Czar, he's proud an' he's great,

But his mind's gane daft wi' the things o' the state ;

He wanted a' Turkey, wi' Russia to keep,

And he thought 't was an easy matter to take.

Doun, doun by Odessa twa auld chiels did dwell,

Wha he thought could just do the thing vera well,

Men-chi-koff by land, Nan-in-koff by sea,

Twa comical coves wi' as queer pedigree.

His fleet was well pouther'd, and maist guid as when new,

He'd plenty o' Cossacks a' clad in grey hue ;

A' the priests said their prayers at a terrible bat,

And wha dare gainsay the auld Czar wi' a' that ?

The ships they weigh'd anchor, and rode cannily

Till they came to the bay of old Sinope,

Where the Moslem fleet lay, as snug as could be,

Just counting one gun to the Muscovites' three.

The auld Capitan Pacha was sipping his wine,

Half his crew were ashore on the spree at the time,

When a seaman sang out, in a voice vera gruff,

" By holy Mahomed ! here comes the Moskoff."

Then the fiery Pacha pu'ed hard his chibouk,

" God is great !" he exclaim'd, his coffee then took,

He counted his beads, then twice scratch'd his head,

" Beat the tambour to quarters," he quietly said.

No fuss did he make, nor excited got he,

Quite firmly convinced in his own destiny ;

Death had no terrors, for this gallant auld Turk

Was not of a breed war's dangers to shirk.

He order'd a broadside as the Ruskies came on,

Which was promptly return'd, wi' interest thereon ;

Though the Moskoffs were threefold in vessels and guns,

No thoughts of surrender had Islam's brave sons.

They fought lang and weel, they fought to the last,

Their vessels went down, wi' their flags on the mast ;

No craven among " Amaum "* that day cried,

" Allah e Allah,"† their war-cry, and wi' it they died.

* Amaum—The Turkish cry for quarter.
† Allah e Allah—The Mussulman's general war cry.

The Ottoman flag-ship at last was blown up,

And the auld Pacha's gane wi' his Hoories* to sup.

O' himself and his crew but small pieces remain,

For the foe show'd no mercy, eternal their shame.

The massacre o'er they dared no' remain,

But set sail at once their harbours to gain ;

For had Britain or France their bull-dogs let loose,

It had soon been all up with the fleet of the Russ.

Retribution though tardy will certainly come,

And vengeance has follow'd the ill deeds they hae done ;

Sevastopol's taken, their fortress laid low,

Their fleet was all sunk without striking a blow.

The Oronoco transport, homeward bound.

* The Hoories are the seventy celestial virgins, ever young and beautiful, who will contribute to the happiness of the Faithful that reach the paradise of Mahomed.

EASTWARD-HO !

> " *King Henry.*—On, on, ye noble English —
> For there is none of you so mean and base,
> That hath not noble lustre in your eyes.
> I see you stand like greyhounds on the slip,
> Straining upon the start—the game's afoot:
> Follow your spirit.
> " *Pistol.*—Touch her soft mouth, and march."
>
> KING HENRY V.

FAREWELL, old friends ! adieu once more ;

　　Ships are heaving on the main,

To bear us from the well-lov'd shore

　　None of us may see again.

To Eastern lands, far o'er the deep,

　　Again we sail to meet the foe ;

Cheer up, my darling—do not weep ;

　　Duty calls, and we must go.

The hour of parting now is nigh,

    Blanch'd is ev'ry soldier's cheek ;

Friends shake hands with many a sigh,

    Veterans even cannot speak.

Cheer up, cheer up, my comrades bold,

    This is not a time to sigh ;

The bloody wolf is in the fold—

    Vengeance now must be the cry.

Hark ! hear you not the signal guns

    Booming o'er the rolling deep ;

Old England calls her gallant sons—

    Cheer up, comrades ! do not weep.

Soldiers must not be heartbroken,

    Ours is not a life to mourn ;

Farewell words are best soon spoken,

    One fond kiss, and we are gone.

THE NEGLECTED SOLDIER.

" Go to the wars, would you? where a man may serve seven years
for the loss of a leg, and have not money enough at the end to buy
him a wooden one?"—PERICLES.

" There's but three of my hundred-and-fifty left alive; and they
are, for the town's end, to beg during life."—KING HENRY IV.

FAME is but a fleeting shadow,

Glory but an empty name;

Spite of all that I have gone through,

'Tis, I find, a losing game.

Without interest, without money,

Nothing can a soldier gain;

Though he be the sole survivor

Of a host of comrades slain.

What avail these glitt'ring honours,

　　Which a Queen laid on my breast;

Though I've sought them from my childhood,

　　Would I'd fallen with the rest.

Then my heart had not been broken,

　　Life had fled without a sigh ;

Hunger presses—I am fainting—

　　Ought a soldier thus to die?

THE END.

LONDON :

PRINTED BY W. CLOWES AND SONS, STAMFORD STREET
AND CHARING CROSS.

OPINIONS OF THE PRESS.

" The Times," 26th December, 1860.

THE HUNTING-GROUNDS OF THE OLD WORLD.

Sporting adventures depend for their interest entirely upon the narrator. If he adds to professional enthusiasm the qualities of a good companion, the public ear is soon gained. The spirit of our Teutonic forefathers is still strong within us, and the charms of a wild life are heightened by the consciousness of interests to which they were strangers. But the "Old Shekarry" is more than a mere executioner of wild beasts. If but half of his stories are true—and we believe every word of them—he is a sportsman of a very rare order. To first-rate marksmanship, undaunted resolution and endurance, he appears to unite great powers of organization, and the faculty of attaching men and even animals to himself. Such characters in rougher times have become "hunters of men," and it is a great pity that even now they are not oftener employed on the "special services" of war. Meanwhile, the feats of our countrymen in far-off jungles and on untrodden mountains are not without their influence in supporting that *prestige* which forms the outworks of national power.

These reminiscences range over the Deccan, Southern India, and Circassia, and conclude with some "Practical hints on Firearms and their use." A greater variety of sporting experiences has probably never fallen to the lot of any one, and the invariable good fortune of the author seems to be of a piece with the "*fortuna populi Romani*"—that success which attends on the old Roman virtues. His first lessons were taken under one "Walter," of whose memory

("for my friend sleeps his last under the shade of a giant forest-tree"\
the "Old Shekarry" always speaks with the deepest reverence. He
was "well known as the most fearless hunter and unerring shot in a
country pre-eminent for the excellence of its sportsmen." The first
chapter contains the account of a day's deer-stalking under his
guidance; the second, an admirable description of a hog-chase, in
which, after all the rest of the field were tailed off, the author con-
tends for the honour of the spear with N——, a celebrated hog-hunter.
"Another moment and the point of my spear was among his bristles;
a touch of the heel, a lift of the bridle, a Chiffney rush, and the
victory was won." The boar, however, charges, and, missing his
mark, rolls over N—— and his horse. After hurrying to the rescue
and despatching the "tusker," our hero returns to his friend. The
scene which follows deserves to be quoted :—

"I found him sitting on the ground, with his face buried in his
hands, in great distress, for his horse was struggling in the agonies of
death a few paces from him. The boar, in charging, had ripped up
his belly, his tushes cutting like a knife, and the intestines, also much
injured, were protruding from the wound. I saw at a glance that it
was a hopeless case, and, tapping N—— on the shoulder, I gave a
significant look to a small pistol that I always carried loaded in my
belt on such occasions, in case of accidents.

"He understood what was passing in my mind, walked up to his
dying *serviteur*, and patted his neck. The poor animal, in spite of his
agony, recognized his master, for he raised himself up partly from the
ground, and rubbed his nose against his shoulder in a most affectionate
manner. N—— kissed his forehead, and, passing his hand across his
eyes rushed into the jungle, saying, 'Do not let him linger.' When
his back was turned I placed the muzzle of my pistol to the suffering
animal's temple, and pulled the trigger—a slight quiver of the body
followed the report, and 'Bidgeley' was dead. N—— cut off some of
the hair of his forelock and tail for a *souvenir*, I slung his saddle and
bridle over Lall Babba's back, and we slowly retraced our way
towards the tents."

Omitting the sketches of the "Old Shekarry's gang" of trackers
and beaters, and the exploits of a Scotch doctor, who plays the part
of Wilson in Lord Dufferin's amusing "Letters," the next campaign is
against a formidable man-eating tiger. After following the trail over
most difficult ground, the party come upon a hideous lair, fresh with
traces of his last victim, before surprising whom " he seemed to have
made the circuit of the village two or three times": —

" This was evidently the hecatomb of the man-eater, for I counted, from skulls and remains of half-eaten bodies, about 23 victims of both sexes, as we could see from their hair, clothes, broken bangles, (armlets), and gold and silver ornaments belonging to native women."

Meanwhile, the population of the whole neighbourhood had been mustered to a grand *battue*. Whatever may be said against a *battue* as a murderous and a mechanical process of destruction, demanding no strength, resource, or instinct on the part of any one but the gamekeeper, it is a totally different proceeding where wild beasts are the game. A vast quantity of these, including several tigers, are driven into isolated jungles, and the surrounding grass is fired, when a tigress suddenly breaks cover and tears a horsekeeper to pieces.

" W—— was much affected at the death of his horsekeeper, for he had been in his service for some years, and had always proved himself a faithful servant. However, as nothing could be done, we retook our station in the line, and the *battue* was continued." The complete list of that day's bag was "two tigers and two cubs, three cheetahs and one cub, three bears and two cubs (one taken alive), five elk, four spotted deer, four pigs (four small squeakers taken alive), one porcupine, and one bull neilghau—total, 32 head of game.

" When we came near our camp the procession was reformed; my gang and some of the Sepoys amused themselves by dancing in front of the dead tigers, before which our guns were carried decked out with flowers, and singing an extemporary song, the burden of which was something to this effect :—' That great and gallant deeds had been performed that day; that four tigers of burnt fathers having eaten dirt, and the brave and generous gentlemen being satisfied with their day's sport, plenty of bucksheesh and inam (rewards and presents) would, as a matter of course, fall to the lot of their well-wishing followers, whose mouths were watering and stomachs panting with the thoughts of how they would be filled by the sheep which the well-known charitable and generously-minded gentlemen would certainly distribute.' The chorus being taken up by the whole party, was something deafening."

Still the man-eater remained at large, and the glory of vanquishing him in single combat was reserved for the " Old Shekarry " himself. Knowing that several post-runners had been carried off by the monster near a particular bend of the road, the author, disregarding the protestations of his gang, provides himself with the jingling rattle of a post-runner and proceeds slowly down the road :—

" While ascending the opposite side of the ravine I heard a slight noise like the crackling of a dry leaf; I paused, and, turning to the left, fronted the spot from whence I thought the noise proceeded. I distinctly saw a movement or waving in the high grass, as if something was making its way towards me; then I heard a loud purring sound, and saw something twitching backwards and forwards behind a clump of low bush and long grass, about eight or ten paces from me, and a little in the rear. It was a ticklish moment, but I felt prepared. I stepped back a couple of paces, in order to get a better view, which action probably saved my life, for immediately the brute sprang into the middle of the road, alighting about six feet from the place where I was standing. I fired a hurried shot ere he could gather himself up for another spring, and when the smoke cleared away I saw him rolling over and over in the dusty road, writhing in his death agony, for my shot had entered the neck and gone downwards into his chest. I stepped on one side and gave him my second barrel behind the ear, when dark blood rushed from his nostrils, a slight tremor passed over all his limbs, and all was still. The man-eater was dead, and his victims avenged."

These personal encounters with wild animals are really the characteristic feature of the volume, and the reader at last takes it as a matter of course that the narrator should "suddenly come face to face upon an immense tiger;" or, after firing at one from an ambuscade dug in the ground, should see the beast leap clean over his head and fall crashing into the bushes behind him. We extract two specimens of hair-breadth escapes such as Van Amburgh might have envied. The first was a *rencontre* with a "huge female bear," rushing down a nullah :—

"I was directly in her path, and, with a roar, she made right at me; I let drive at her head with my only barrel that had not been discharged, but it failed to stop her, and she had knocked me down and was on me in the twinkling of an eye.

"The slope of the hill was steep, and we both of us rolled over and over several times. I was almost breathless, when Googooloo rushed on her with his billhook and endeavoured to attract her attention. Luckily she could not bite at all, as my shot had smashed her snout and lower jaw to pieces; but she kept me locked in her embrace, and squeezed me more roughly than affectionately.

"My head was well protected with a bison-skin cap; and getting a tight grasp of her fur on each side, with my arms underneath hers, so that she could not do me much injury with her claws, I regularly wrestled with her for some time; and, although I brought my science to play, and threw her on her back several times ' by giving her the leg,' she never let go her hug, and I was almost suffocated with the quantity of blood and froth that came from her wound and covered my face, beard, and chest.

" Googooloo made frantic hits at her from time to time with his bill-hook (the only weapon he had, having lent D—— his knife), but I ordered him to desist, as his blows did not appear to do the bear much harm, and I was afraid of catching one. At last Bruin appeared to be getting weaker, and I saw her wounds and loss of blood were telling; and after a little trouble I managed to draw my knife, and drove it up to the hilt in her body under the armpits. She gave me an ugly hug, and fell over on her side, pulling me with her. It was her last effort, and I picked myself up quite out of puff, but not much injured, having only received a slight claw on the loins and another rather more severe on the instep. I drew my pistol, which I could not manage to get at before, to give her a settler, but it was not re-quired—the game was over, my antagonist was dead."

The other was in a similar situation, but the antagonist was an ele-phant which was struck by a " shot four inches too low. It failed to stop him, and before I could get out of the way, the huge brute was on me; I saw something dark pass over me, felt a severe blow, and found myself whizzing through the air; then all was oblivion." While the author was lying stunned and bleeding, the elephant turned upon Googooloo, who escaped by swinging himself up by the hanging branch of a tree :—

" The elephant, balked of his victim, rushed wildly backwards and forwards two or three times, as if searching for him, and then, with a hoarse scream of disappointment, came tearing down the bed of the nullah. I was directly in his path, and powerless to get out of the way. A moment more and I saw that I was perceived, for down he charged on me with a fiendish roar of vengeance. With difficulty I raised my rifle, and, taking a steady aim between his eyes, pulled the trigger—it was my only chance. When the smoke cleared away, I perceived a mighty mass lying close to me. At last I had conquered. Soon after this I must have sunk in a swoon, for I hardly remember anything until I found myself lying in my hut, and B—— leaning over me."

One cannot help admiring the adroitness with which this accom-plished strategist shifts his tactics. Once he creeps up behind an ele-phant and disables him from charging by firing two barrels up his raised leg; at another time he shoots an enormous fish with a ramrod, having a log-line attached to it. Now he awaits and drops, at six paces' distance, a bull-bison, much larger than the one which now stands in the Strand as a trophy of Mr. Berkeley's prowess, being 19 hands high at the shoulder; now he stabs to death a wild bull, 16 hands high, which had just capsized himself and his horse. A tigress strikes down "poor Ali, who, notwithstanding my orders, had separated himself from the rest. Although I felt I was too late to save him, I determined he should be amply revenged," and accordingly the infuriated animal is despatched with a single shot. K—— is chased by an elephant, and "would have had no chance if he had not been able to dodge him by running round trees. I could not, for the moment, get a fair shot at any vulnerable part; but, seeing that the elephant had got so near that he could almost have reached him with his trunk, I let drive a double shot at his ear, and brought him to his knees, which gave K—— time to clamber up into a tree. It was a very near touch, for he was breathless, and another few seconds would have seen him trampled under foot; as it was, I was able to despatch the tusker with my second gun, which Googooloo handed me just as he began to recover himself and was getting on his knees."

We have no space for the death-scenes of the Neilgherry tiger and the Circassian bear, though among the most spirited descriptions in the volume, or for the *ruse* by which he turns the superstitions of his followers to account in overcoming the dread of the malaria on the Anamulai Mountains. Nothing seems to come amiss to him. If he loses his game over a precipice, he submits to be dangled down by a rope till he reaches the ledge on which it is lying. If his baggage-pony is carried off by Circassian banditti, he overtakes them while their trail is yet fresh, recovers the stolen goods by a *coup de main*, brands his prisoners with a heated horse-shoe, and turns them adrift into the forest. The ascent of the El-Bruz, which follows, deserves the attention of the Alpine Club, especially as the higher summit was after all left unscaled, being cut off, like the peak of Chimborazo, from the accessible side by an impassable chasm.

Most pursuits, ardently followed out, contain in themselves the elements of an education. The "Old Shekarry" writes like a man whose character owes much to forest-life. A sincere devotion to his art elevates him into a kind of troubadour of hunting crusades; gives true eloquence to his pictures of forest-scenery, and no mean grace to the improvised songs with which he was wont to beguile the evenings after a day's sport. The associations of the tournament predominate over those of the shambles. We can forgive a little egotism, a little unnecessary dialogue, and a little Byronic affectation for the sake of the great literary merits of the works. It shows us what the life of Mr. Asshcton Smith confirms, that a consummate sportsman is made of no ordinary stuff. But it presumes, as a condition of success, a degree of labour and patience amounting almost to self-sacrifice. "M. Jules Gérard spent upwards of *six hundred nights* in the forest before he killed his twenty-sixth lion." The "Old Shekarry" himself was engaged for days together under an Indian sun in following some one quarry, resolutely abstaining from all inferior game. In the valuable hints on rifle-shooting which close the volume he betrays no leaning to short cuts and empirical expedients. "Constant practice," "intense study," and close attention to the regulation system of instruction, are the only secrets of his method. At the same time he declares for the breech-loading principle, and the reasons by which he justifies this preference in the case of fowling-pieces pp. 488-96) seem to us unanswerable. The man who can knock over an ibex at 400 yards, and meets the fiercest animals single-handed and on foot, has a right to speak on these points.

The "Old Shekarry" represents a class of men with which a country that owns a hundred colonies cannot afford to dispense. The race of "mighty hunters" is not extinct; their descendants are the pioneers of many an enterprise of commercial or scientific discovery. Nor is the most ancient of human occupations robbed of its dignity when it is associated with the tastes of a scholar and the feelings of a gentleman.

"BELL'S LIFE," 3rd June, 1860.

THERE is a general impression among the reading public that a work almost entirely devoted to sporting, more especially to the actual narration of sporting events which have occurred in the experience of one individual, must be, to a certain extent, a monotonous chronicle of carnage; and this impression is justified by the majority of works on the subject. But, as there is no rule without exception, the minority do from time to time vindicate, and most pleasantly so, the perfect feasibility of this material, in itself at the time so interesting to everybody taking part in it, being made almost equally interesting to those who have not; and our author in his present work has assuredly well entitled himself to be ranked high among that glorious minority.

His qualifications being, however, first, true sportsmanship, with its indispensable attribute, great powers of observation, combined with, secondly, an easy, graceful, and gentlemanlike faculty of expressing his ideas, must have gone far towards making his task feasible (we will not detract from his merits, looking, moreover, at the numbers who have tried and failed in the same line, by saying an easy one); but when we add to the other qualifications, thirdly, the power of illustrating by his own spirited pencil the most stirring incidents which he has met with in flood and field, possessed by "The Old Shekarry," we may fairly wonder the less at his success. As in true sportsmanship must be included, as the principal ingredient, humanity, the charge of chronicling butchery page after page is disposed of at once; and as an easy and graceful style of writing presupposes a considerable degree of humour and pleasantry, we find matter of fact in this volume quite free from monotony; and as in the sporting events marked by the finger-post of plates, of which the only complaint can be that they are not more numerous, the interest of every reader must be well supported, especially when the softer feelings are appealed to by such descriptions as that of the death of the hog-hunter's horse, Bidgeley; so in the intermediate spaces—such as the stories of the Scotch Indian, who paves the way to getting the Begum to treat our sportsman with a nautch by dosing her well beforehand with stiff gin-and-water, with all the attendant incidents of this Caledonian Machiavelli's interview with her highness—the readers, whether sportsmen or not, will be difficult to amuse if they fail to be tickled by such passages as that just referred to.

Modesty, also another attribute of the real sportsman, shows itself throughout, in the grateful manner in which "H. A. L." acknowledges the services and assistance rendered him by his native attendants, whose attachment to him speaks volumes, both for the kindness which conciliated them and the good management which kept them up to their ardour and discipline, without his having otherwise to boast of his own deeds to secure these most necessary points for a successful foray against the wild animals of the jungles.

Another very pleasing feature in this book is the circumstance that, wherever much game was killed at once, it seems to have been, not for the mere purpose of collecting trophies, except in the case of ivory, but for the support of his followers and the native tribes who accompanied them, or for the absolute preservation of human life; as also the fact that the most noble of beasts—the elephant—can be, by *good shooting, and a proper knowledge of the point at which to aim*, put to death without the awful cannonading, and consequently protracted misery to the majestic victim, which less skilful hunters have had to employ, and thus given their readers the painful, though we are heartily glad to find *false*, impression that it was unavoidable to inflict an awful amount of suffering before bringing to bay the grandest quarry that the animal kingdom affords to the hunter.

With these hurried remarks, which want of space alone prevents our adding largely to, we leave the work with the greatest confidence to the reading world in general, and in particular to that portion of it who are smitten with the *ardor renaticus*, as the most interesting, as well as instructive, production of the kind which has appeared since the days of the immortal Nimrod.

"SATURDAY REVIEW," *June 16th*, 1860.

"H. A. L.'s" book is exceedingly amusing, and its blemishes are very few and very pardonable.

"THE ATHENÆUM," *September 1*, 1860.

THE "Old Shekarry" not only leads us through the great forests of the south of India, and over the plains of the Deccan, but presents us with other multiform experiences; wandering now into the mountains of Circassia, and now to the African plains. The "Old Shekarry" has many things to tell us which have no smack of the shambles in them. In one of his forest rambles he encountered specimens of the wild races who live in trees, deep in the recesses of the mighty Indian jungles, and who seem to have nothing human but the name of man.

After a life of adventure in the far East, it is no wonder that our Author sought in the Crimea a renewal of excitement. When pale peace again made its unwelcome appearance, he betook himself once more to the hunting-grounds; and wandering into Circassia, adventured the ascent of the giant mountain El-Bruz.

OPINIONS OF THE PRESS.

The reader will pass with satisfaction to a very sensible chapter on breech-loaders and rifle practice, with which the work concludes. On such a subject, the authority of such a writer is great; and we are glad to have our own opinion confirmed as to the superiority of the new weapons, and the breech-loading improvement generally. For the rest, the volunteer may glean some useful hints from a writer who speaks of Hythe with more than Hythe experience.

"THE OBSERVER," *May* 28, 1860.

THE Author of this work describes himself as "a wanderer over many lands;" and, it may be added, that he is also a "mighty hunter." The volume is a pleasing record of feats of daring and dexterity in the pursuit of wild animals, and will well repay perusal on the part of all lovers of field-sports on a large scale.

"THE NEW SPORTING MAGAZINE," *August*, 1860.

WE should recommend our modern Nimrods, if they wish for real excitement, to pack up their traps, take the overland route and try their hands at drawing the noble game inhabiting the jungles of India. There they will have hunting worthy of their great proto-type, Nimrod the First, and to which hare or fox hunting is child's-play, and a steeplechase a senseless pursuit of a broken neck.

First of all, however, let him get the "Old Shekarry's" work, and read it carefully, weighing well the dangers of the enterprise, or they may find their courage fail them when the pinch comes.

This most interesting work is full of such incidents; changing the game from tigers to elephants, bears, bisons, deer, elks, wild boars, panthers, and other smaller game, with a variety of anecdotes, illustrative both of high and low life in India, Circassia, and Algeria, for our Nimrod has also paid these countries a sporting visit. We cannot go into particulars, but can honestly recommend the book to all true lovers of field-sports, as a genuine and interesting work on a subject that has hitherto only been touched on by travellers in the countries to which it refers.

OPINIONS OF THE PRESS.

"THE ERA."

No sportsman can read this work without considerable profit; and every one will be struck with the sound truthfulness of this mighty hunter's descriptions of the wild denizens of the forest, and the piquant pictures he draws of " the pleasures of the pathless woods."

"THE REVIEW," *June* 9, 1860.

AN agreeable surprise will await the reader, who, not being addicted to field-sports, may chance to open the volume of which we now propose to enter upon a critical notice, and which, though faithful to the promise implied in its title, abounds in stirring adventures of the chase; appeals largely, also, to a wide range of tastes; and embraces within its contents, a varied fund of interest and information.

Thus in the three fields of sporting activity to which the Author introduces us—India, Circassia, and Algeria—not content with a bare narrative of his marvellous exploits with gun or spear, he often expatiates on striking descriptions of the beauties of nature, or sketches the manners and habits of wild races of men, which he diversifies again with descriptions of towns, and of the softer pleasures there in vogue; paints the voluptuous allurements of oriental life; delineates the grandeur and the grace of the ancient architecture in those interesting regions; and interweaves all that can captivate the fancy or instruct the mind, into his discursive story. There are traits of humour, also, for the reader intent on amusement: tragic incident and tale for more serious dispositions; and poetry both gay and pathetic for the refined admirer of the muse.

It is among the mountain heights, however, and the immemorial forests that our author, though nothing comes amiss to him, is most at home; and he communicates his experience of the sublimities and beauties of landscape scenery with a freshness and vigour that speak his keen sense of enjoyment and ardent sympathies with the glories of creation. Imagination, taste, and sentiment largely pervade the whole composition. As for the sporting performances related in the work, they are truly astonishing, and fill the mind with horror by the perilous character that they assume. Who does not feel an uneasy sensation as he accompanies our author to the tiger's lair, strewed thick with the remains of mutilated victims, with human bones, and the trinkets of the native women devoured by the wild beast? What heart is not turned in its beat, as the same fearless sportsman is hugged by a bear; or, as he dangles by a silken rope, in his descent of the yawning precipice, to recover from a ledge of rock the ibex that he has killed with his unerring rifle. These and the like exciting events are powerfully told, and will arrest the attention of the least inquisitive.

The chase is, indeed, the image of war, when the most ferocious of the animal tribes constitute the game, and the perpendicular height is to be scaled, or the foaming torrent crossed, in quest of the noble sport. There is need for circumspection at every step, when the slightest error or over-sight may be irremediable and fatal; and the discipline of mind and body cannot but be of the most salutary character, when vigilance, caution, fertility of resource, coolness, and courage are all required to circumvent and conquer the wary and formidable monsters, against whom the brute strength of man is wholly unavailing. It is a real war that is to be waged with an enemy worthy of human prowess, and taxing some of the finest qualities to the utmost. What better school can be found for the soldier to practise during peace—the stratagems and arts of war? And what is more likely to sharpen his courage and confidence, on which at such a time must be his main reliance? Add to these exciting pursuits a practical knowledge of military evolutions and tactics, and a proper sense of subordination to authority, and the elements most indispensable to a soldier will be complete.

The practical part of the work which gives rise to these comments is also calculated to be extremely useful, and must not pass without notice. Here the sportsman will find rules as to dress and baggage, and vehicles and beasts of burden, and general accoutrements and utensils, as to provisions and ammunition, and, above all, as to weapons, which will be eminently serviceable to him in taking the field amidst the primæval forests and pathless mountains, where auxiliary or extraneous assistance is out of the question, and a man must depend upon his own forethought and ingenuity to avoid or to extricate himself from the numerous accidents that beset him in his adventurous course. The volume is concluded by a clear, vigorous, and interesting treatise of a theoretical and practical nature, on muzzle-loading and breech-loading arms, and rifle-shooting, with remarks on uniform, the whole of which deserves the earnest attention, not only of the sportsman but of the professional soldier and the volunteer.

As our author is of a very observing turn of mind, he frequently describes the appearance and dimensions, and likewise the habits of the animals that he kills, and indulges in graphic sketches of the trees and vegetation of the tropics, so that the lover of natural history will be gratified, not, indeed, with a profound, but a popular and pleasing account of animal and vegetable life. In general, it is in quest of game that our author explores the picturesque grandeur or beauty of primitive nature; but sometimes the thirst of daring enterprise, and the admiration of towering mountains, leads him far above the haunts of bird or beast, to regions in which the awful glacier, resplendent with rainbow colours, opens its treacherous chasms, and the thunder of the avalanche makes sublime and appalling music, amidst the toppling crags and the precipitous rocks. The Caucasus is the scene of this exploit, and El-Bruz the mountain which, at imminent risk, and with the actual loss, in returning, of one of his attendants, our author ascends.

It is a book of sports and a book of travels in one—of sports the most noble and useful, because they are directed chiefly against the most destructive of animals; and of travels the most interesting, because the delineation of the objects of nature and art is interspersed with "hair-breadth escapes" and the most alarming personal dangers.

At a future day we purpose to return to the volume before us, which, let us not omit to add, is in point of paper and topography well worthy of its agreeable contents, and is illustrated by a series of tinted lithographs that bring before the eye our daring sportsman's encounters with wild beasts. The frontispiece (from a photograph), and its duplicate representation in gilt on the binding of the book, are very appropriate, as the open jaws of the tiger symbolize a principal topic of the work; and interior and exterior are calculated to render it an ornament to any library.

www.ingramcontent.com/pod-product-compliance
Lightning Source LLC
Chambersburg PA
CBHW020609030726
47497CB00007B/2153